Murder at the Wine Cave

A READ BETWEEN THE WINES COZY MYSTERY SERIES
BOOK FOUR

DANI SIMMS

TRILLIUM SAGE

ISBN | Ebook: 978-1-958118-18-4

ISBN | Print: 978-1-958118-20-7

To RJS...

I love you more than you love adventuring.

Chapter One

It was a beautiful day that Friday, and it was quickly turning into an even more beautiful evening. To Avery, that meant all the makings of a spectacular Saturday ahead of her. It also meant that the entire town of Los Robles was celebrating the start of the weekend.

The road had been rocky, but Avery felt proud as she handed the invitation to the opening of her new tasting area to Marcus, the man who owned the vineyard next to her own. She hadn't gone alone, either.

The women of the Stammtisch were right there with her, and they had made a day of it. When Avery's mother had talked her into joining the Stammtisch, she hadn't known that such a gathering was even a *thing*. However, in the end, an informal gathering of women was precisely what she needed, and she had become a permanent part of the group since. The women had quickly become Avery's best friends.

"Well, now that he has his invitation, why don't we sample some wine?" Deb suggested.

Avery was eager for a wine tasting, and it was why she'd insisted that they all took a cab to the vineyard. Normally, Avery didn't enjoy gossip, but Deb always did have a great way of telling a story, and she couldn't help but wonder what kind of gossip Deb had in store for them that day.

"Of course!" Eleanor chimed in. "I already ordered our tasting when we walked through the door!" Eleanor laughed. She was certainly the organizer of the group. There was hardly an event that she didn't arrange and all of them had been fun.

"Let me be seated, then," Tiffany added.

Avery sat down next to Tiffany, where she was most comfortable. She'd known Tiffany the longest given they'd been childhood friends. Tiffany was also the newest member of the Stammtisch and had recently taken a job as Avery's assistant at Le Blanc Cellars.

On the other side of the table, Camille sat quietly and watched the world unfold around her. That was how she always was. Occasionally, she would say something, and it would take everyone by surprise.

However, on the days that she couldn't make it, her absence was felt deeply by all. Avery had never had that many friends before. She felt pleased with her life at that point, and she felt as if she was finally learning to live without her husband.

A boating accident had taken him from her, and she'd assumed she would never feel better again. The sadness had never left, but she was enjoying life again, and she felt then that she had more purpose than ever before.

Sometimes, late at night, that thought made her sad too. But every time that she spent the day, or even an hour, with the friends she had made, she found herself forgetting her own sadness.

Their glasses had almost emptied when Marcus, the owner of the vineyard approached their table.

"Are you ladies perhaps interested in a private tour of the estate?" he asked.

"Of course!" Avery answered without hesitation. She'd been

eager to see what other businesses like hers had been up to and how they functioned.

"Not with an empty glass, though," Eleanor responded in a typical fashion.

"Of course not," Marcus smiled.

Within moments their glasses were filled, and they were being led through the vineyard to marvel at the views and modern structures.

The women admired the beautiful pink shades of the sky that blanketed the glory of the vineyards. They had been fortunate to be there right as the sun was setting as if a show had been put on just for them.

"Perhaps you and Charles should come here for your date," Tiffany said, reminding the rest of the women that Avery had accepted the offer of a date.

They gladly took the opportunity to tease her relentlessly for it. Charles worked in the wine room at Avery's vineyard, Le Blanc Cellars. They'd become close friends, but it seemed that their friendship had the potential for something more.

Avery had taken herself by surprise when she had accepted his offer, as she had never considered a life without her husband. But fate had other plans, and he was no longer there with her.

She hadn't thought about the date much and was trying not to. They hadn't set a day and time yet, but she knew he would eventually ask. It just felt to her that there was still so much she needed to think about.

Then, every time she felt that way, she would hear her husband's voice remind her that the best things in life need little thought at all. This meant that either it wasn't a good idea or she needed to stop thinking about it. She couldn't quite decide which one of those explanations she preferred.

They walked through the vines and came upon a small building. It was modern and painted black. Marcus smiled knowingly as he opened the door and ushered them in.

"This is my private collection," he said proudly.

The women gasped when they were met with one of the largest wine collections Avery had ever seen. She knew some of the bottles and understood exactly how expensive they were.

The room was built to keep a steady temperature, and it was pristinely clean.

"How many bottles are there?" Deb asked, looking for her next bit of interesting information to share with the rest of the world.

"Just over one thousand," Marcus answered. "And I plan to build another room just like this one."

"It's the most beautiful thing I have ever seen," Eleanor joked as she sipped her wine.

The women walked along the rows of bottles as they cast their glances over the labels. Avery had never been much of a collector, but collections of any kind always impressed her.

She was impressed by his vineyard in general. It did not make her love her own vineyard any less—they were simply very different. His was modern with sleek lines and colors. Her vineyard felt a little more comfortable than that.

Marcus watched proudly as the women gawked over some of the expensive bottles in his collection.

"This is one of my favorites," he said softly.

Avery looked up and saw that he held an old bottle of Le Blanc wine. It was one of their greatest wines, and Avery hadn't seen one of those bottles in quite some time. She smiled as he slipped the wine back on the shelf.

"I have one more place to show you if you'd like to see it," Marcus said loudly.

The women stopped to look at him, and he got an excited, cheeky look on his face.

"It's not somewhere that I often show on these tours, but you ladies have such great energy on such a beautiful day. I'd love to show you the wine cave," he explained.

"Now that sounds exciting!" Deb sang.

They stopped on their way to the wine cave to have their glasses filled again, and by the time they approached the entrance, the five of them were all a little tipsy.

They giggled easily and struggled over the cobblestones. Marcus laughed too as he sipped on his own glass.

He welcomed them inside the cave, which was large and ominous. It had a completely different feeling to the rest of the vineyard. It was old and gloomy, and there were no modern or sleek lines in sight.

The large barrels lined the space which seemed to continue on forever. As they walked, Avery noticed some large leather sofas placed in certain spaces with bookshelves around them.

"Do you have functions in here?" she asked.

Marcus shrugged. "Rarely, but that was the initial plan."

"Did it not work out?" Avery pressed.

It made no sense to her that people wouldn't be interested in that kind of space for their functions. It was large and beautiful, and it seemed like nothing else in the area.

"It feels too special to me to have strangers come in here," Marcus said plainly. "This is the heart of the vineyard, and it feels almost sacred."

Eleanor did an excellent job of pulling his attention away with her questions. Avery didn't mind. Her social battery was running dangerously low, and she was looking for any reason to sneak off on her own somewhere.

She approached one space that had large leather chairs and a bookshelf. Avery was curious to see what kind of books would occupy a bookshelf like that. She found, instead, rows of books with no titles.

It was odd to her, and she walked along the rows, searching for anything with writing on it. Then, she saw something shining above one of the books. She bent down to take a look and spotted a small door handle among the books.

The corners of her mouth turned up into a smile. It was a door, cleverly disguised as a beautiful bookshelf stocked with books. Avery wanted to take a photograph, so she reached into her bag to grab her phone.

But between the glass, the zipper of her bag, and her own clumsiness, she dropped her phone, and it slid across the floor. With it fell her lip balm that had accidentally been pulled out along with her phone.

The lip balm rolled right across the floor and slipped behind a cabinet. Avery sighed. To most people, a lip balm was nothing important. To Avery, it was her favorite lip balm. When she'd found it, she had bought five. That was her last one.

Avery placed her glass down on a nearby coffee table and approached the cabinet to search for her lip balm. It couldn't have gone far and was likely wedged between the cabinet and the wall.

However, when she got there, she noted there was a significant amount of space between the back of the cabinet and the wall. She chalked it up to the unevenness of the cave wall and focused instead on finding the lip balm.

She stuck her hand into the dark space, hoping she wouldn't find a rat or anything as awful. She reached around on the floor. It would not have been surprising to her if she had found some dust or a paper that had been lost behind there.

Instead, she felt something a little harder. It was rounded and felt like leather. It wasn't her lip balm, so she continued her search, working her hand over the hard leather object.

Her fingers began to feel sore. At that point, she pulled her hand away and decided on another approach. She pushed the side of her head to the wall and attempted to see between the space.

If she could spot it, then she'd know how far she needed to reach to get it. Whatever she did, she had to get it back, and she had to be careful. The cabinet was filled with crystal glasses, and she couldn't imagine the colossal noise and major embarrass-ment if she knocked it over.

The lip balm was good, but it wasn't *that* good.

Still, she wanted to give it at least one more try. But it was too dark to see. So, she reached for her phone again, checked it for scratches, and then pushed all the buttons until she found the one that turned on the flashlight.

When the little light lit up, she sighed a breath of relief. Avery placed her head against the wall again and held up her phone to fill the space with light. She was certain she'd spot her lip balm somewhere nearby.

But when the light filled the space, she was met rather by the cold gray eyes of a man, wedged between the cabinet and the wall. Unfortunately for Avery, they had no life left in them.

She had hoped to find her lip balm. Instead, she found a dead body.

Chapter Two

Avery's scream echoed through the wine cave as she stumbled backward, tripping over the corner of a rug. The sound of her scream was followed closely by the sound of running footsteps as the rest of the group came to look for her.

Avery fell, landing hard against the ground as everyone ran to help her. It felt as if her breath was getting stuck in her throat. She couldn't find a voice with which to speak. But she could see the concern on everyone's faces.

Although the only sound she could hear was the sound of her own heart thumping in her ears, she knew they were asking her what had happened. She didn't know what else to do, so she held out her hand and pointed at the space between the cabinet and the wall. Her hand was shaking, and she tried her best not to look again. Her phone with the flashlight still on was lying on the floor next to the cabinet, and this time she was certain the screen had cracked.

Marcus picked up the phone and shone the light into the space. She watched as his body language changed. His back straightened, and he took a few steps back.

"What's back there?" Deb pleaded as she brushed Avery's hair out of her face.

Marcus looked at them. His face was pale, and he swallowed hard.

"Th...there's a dead body behind that cabinet," he said with his voice barely above a whisper.

Within a second, Eleanor pulled Avery up off the ground and ushered her outside. The rest of the women followed with Marcus close behind. When Avery could catch her breath, she phoned Chief Mathers and told him to get there as soon as possible.

When he arrived, she was happy to see him. She'd come to know him as a man she could trust. He arrived with a team of officers who wasted no time closing off the scene.

Marcus sat at Avery's side while the Stammtisch women handed both of them a full glass of wine. Avery sipped gratefully at it as she tried hard not to blink. Every time she blinked, she saw the cold lifeless eyes staring back at her again.

"We have some questions for all of you," a police officer said, interrupting them.

"Of course," Avery said.

"Chief Mathers would like to question you two himself," the officer said. "But the rest of you can follow me."

The women obliged. Everyone was shaken up, and a beautiful day had quickly become a terrible night. Once they were led away, Avery and Marcus sat in silence as they sipped their wine.

"I don't even know where to begin," Marcus said. "I have no idea what to tell the police or what I'm supposed to do tomorrow."

Avery smiled. "You'll be alright," she said. "They'll ask the questions they need to. Just make sure you answer as honestly as possible. And you can face tomorrow when you get there."

"What do I do with all of this?" he asked, waving at the wine cave.

"It is likely going to be awhile before they let you back in there," she said.

Marcus sank his head into his hand as he tried to soothe his growing headache. Avery knew how he was feeling; she had seen what he saw, and it was unlikely that either of them would get any sleep that night.

"Do you know him?" she asked.

"Know who?" he mumbled.

"The man behind the cabinet," she answered. "Do you know the dead man?"

Marcus shook his head. "I've never seen him before. I wonder how long he's been there."

"Well, it didn't smell in there, so it couldn't have been long," she said. "How did you wind up with the body of a stranger tucked behind your cabinet?" She asked the question knowing that he wouldn't have an answer for her. But neither of them was able to think entirely straight. It was a tricky conversation, but she didn't want to sit in silence anymore. She opted, rather, for some kind of distraction.

"I've been asking myself that this entire time," he said. "There are many staff members who have access to the wine cave. Until now, it's been one of my favorite places on this vineyard, but now it will be haunted."

"Haunted?" Avery repeated in question.

"Yes, if not by his physical spirit, then by the memory of tonight," he answered solemnly. "I don't think I'll be back here anytime soon. It is a pity."

He turned to look back at the cave. There were flashing lights all around them that lit up the sky.

"That is not a good view," he said quietly.

Avery felt terribly for Marcus. She didn't know him well, as he was only a new acquaintance, but she knew how he felt at that moment. She knew how awful it was. When Chief Mathers walked back out of the wine cave, Avery felt a small amount of relief.

She was happy to see him, despite the serious look of concern on his face. He looked tired and stressed and as if he had some bad news. He approached them and, despite the dire circumstances, gave them both a friendly smile.

"Thank you for answering my call," Avery said when he reached them.

"Of course," he said. "You must be Marcus."

Marcus nodded and gave his hand for a feeble attempt at a handshake.

"Well, situations like these are never good," Chief Mathers said. "We're going to try and get this over with as soon as possible. The other ladies have answered their questions and have been escorted home."

"Thank you," Avery said, relieved.

"I still need to talk to the two of you, though," he said. "As I am sure you can understand, I have many questions. I just need to piece together what happened here today."

Marcus nodded and stood up. Chief Mathers instructed Avery to wait for him and ushered Marcus to the side. His hands were shaking, and he was pale with fear. She could see how distraught he was by their discovery.

Despite all of that, he seemed to answer all of Chief Mathers' questions easily and without struggle.

After a few minutes, it was Avery's turn. She and Chief Mathers walked a short way out into the vines.

"How are you doing?" Chief Mathers asked.

"I've been better," she teased. "I'm a little stressed."

"That's entirely understandable," he said with a smile. "Run me through it. What happened?"

"I was looking for my lip balm behind the cabinet when I found the body," she said, reliving a terrible moment. "I got such a fright that I screamed and fell. That's when I pointed it out to Marcus."

"What were you all doing in the wine cave?" Chief Mathers asked. "I've been here many times, and I never knew this cave even existed."

"Oh, Marcus was giving us a personal tour of the vineyard," Avery explained. "I was bringing him an invitation to the pond event."

"Ah, yes," Chief Mathers said. "You can note that I will be attending. I got my invitation; thank you."

"That's great," Avery said.

It felt odd to talk about such normal things when they were dealing with something as serious as death.

"Do you think he got trapped?" Avery asked.

Chief Mathers shook his head. "Unlikely," he answered. "If he'd gotten stuck he'd have called out for help. Most likely he was already dead when he was placed behind that cabinet."

Avery felt dizzy. "It's a murder," she said sadly.

"Are you sure you're alright?" Chief Mathers asked.

Avery nodded. "Yes, just a bit shaken up," she answered. "But I'm worried about Marcus. He doesn't seem to be taking it well, and I think the rest of the women might be upset for quite some time."

"There really is no way to recover from something like this," Chief Mathers said. "It is unfortunate, but who knows how much worse it might have been if you didn't find him today. It's a terrible thing to say, but the body is in good condition, which is good for us."

"I suppose that is a good thing, yes," Avery said.

Chief Mathers smiled so kindly at her she almost reached out and hugged him. But her urge to do so was cut short when from over Charles' shoulder she saw the body being carried out. Thankfully, the body was covered, and she could no longer see those dead eyes. But right there, within her sight, was the body of a man who should still have been alive.

"Is there anything I can do for you?" Chief Mathers asked.

Avery swallowed hard. "No, thank you.. I think I'm as alright as I can be, for now."

"Okay, I just have a few more questions for you," he said.

"Of course, go ahead."

Chief Mathers cleared his throat. "How well do you know Marcus?"

Avery shrugged. "I just met him today. It was just a good day, and I guess he was in a good mood and gave us all a tour."

"I see," he said, taking notes. "And you've never been to this vineyard before?"

"No, never," she answered.

"You've never met him, but you wanted to give him an invitation?" he asked.

Avery nodded. "Yes, I figured it would be good to have other business owners attend the opening of the new tasting area. I've been going to businesses all week to take the invitation. Since it is Friday, I thought I would make an event of it and invite the women of the Stammtisch to come with me."

"Sounds like a fun day!"

"It was supposed to be," Avery mumbled.

"I need to ask Marcus some more questions but stay here. There's something I want to talk to you about afterward," he said.

With that, he walked back toward Marcus. Avery didn't know what Chief Mathers wanted to talk about, but she was certain it was important. She wanted to go home, take a hot shower, and wash the day from her skin.

She wanted to crawl into bed with Sprinkles and pretend as if the day had never happened. Avery wanted nothing to do with it anymore, but she knew she needed to stay there.

Chief Mathers wrapped things up with Marcus, and Avery

watched as he was allowed to leave. She was jealous of him as he walked back toward his home.

"Now that the initial questions are all taken care of, I have another question for you. It's a little change of topic, though," he said.

Avery was desperate for a change of subject. "Please, go ahead," she said, forcing a smile.

"What do you think about Charles sending through an application to join the force again?" he asked.

Avery's mouth fell open. "I didn't know he did." she said.

Chief Mathers covered his eyes with his hand. "Oh, dear, I assumed you'd know! The two of you are pretty close, aren't you?"

"Yeah," Avery said. "But he didn't tell me about that! When did he send it?"

"Last week," Chief Mathers said. "I was surprised to see it but happy. He was a good detective when he worked with me. He'd be a great addition to the team."

Avery couldn't believe it. He'd done it without telling her. It didn't seem like something Charles would do, and she wasn't sure how to feel about it. Chief Mathers was right—she and Charles were close. They had only become closer.

They'd been part of most of each other's big decisions for quite some time. Avery couldn't understand why he wouldn't have told her about something so drastic in his life.

Chapter Three

Avery closed the front door behind her and patted an eager Sprinkles on the head. He was happy to see her, and his tail wagged excitedly. But she couldn't match his energy that night.

What was meant to be an easy, relaxing day had turned into a tiresome and stressful event. Although she wanted to get right into bed and sleep and forget about it all, she also wanted to talk to someone.

That person was Charles. Avery had questions for him, and she wouldn't mind the distraction. At least that way the last thought on her mind when she went to bed wouldn't be about the dead body she had found.

The phone rang for all of ten seconds before he answered.

"How are you doing?" he asked solemnly. "Mathers let me know."

Avery sighed. "I'm alright. I'm home, and I'm tired, but I don't really want to talk about it more."

Charles chuckled. "That's alright," he said. "We can talk about it another time. As long as you're alright."

"I'm okay," Avery said. She couldn't help but smile. "But I have to ask you something."

"Anything you want," Charles said cheerfully.

She was almost certain he didn't know what she was going to ask him about. He wouldn't have sounded so cheerful about it if he did.

"Chief Mathers told me you applied to rejoin the force," she said plainly. "Why didn't you tell me about this?"

There was silence on the other end of the line for a brief few seconds.

"I'm sorry I didn't tell you," he relented. "I guess I didn't tell you because I don't know if I really want it yet."

"But you've applied?" she asked.

"Yeah," he answered. "I was thinking about it a lot, and I couldn't come to a decision, so I decided to just send the message to Mathers and take it from there. That doesn't mean I'll do it, though."

"I see," she answered.

It was a surprise to her; she hadn't thought he'd go back. He spoke about his past on the police force before, but only about how tired it had made him. Avery had assumed it meant he hadn't enjoyed it.

"I guess I didn't want to tell you about it until I had made a decision," Charles said.

"That's okay," Avery said in a friendly manner. "I understand. Besides, I am your boss. It's pretty normal to apply for other jobs and not tell your boss about it."

Charles chuckled. "You're also my friend," he said. "And you're not like the other bosses."

"Oh, I hope not!" Avery laughed. "I've had some pretty terrible bosses before."

"Me too," Charles admitted.

"So, how long have you been considering rejoining the force?" she asked.

Avery struggled into her pajamas as she held the phone to her ear. She didn't want to be in her jeans anymore. She was too tired, but she still wanted to talk to him. However, she wasn't prepared to wait until the call was over before she was in her pajama pants.

"It's been on my mind for a couple of weeks now," Charles said. "I mean no offense by this, but I always felt like being an officer of some kind gave me purpose."

"You can't solve any crimes working in the wine room," Avery teased. "And people will taste wine without you too, I suppose. But I'm not sure they'll leave with as much. You're an excellent salesman."

Charles laughed. "It's not me selling the wine," he said. "The *wine* sells the wine!"

"I beg to differ," she argued. "It's the same wine it's always been, and our sales have never been this high."

"That's because you're in charge," he said. "I don't know...I think I was hoping that when Mathers came back to me with his decision, I could make a choice then. You never know. Maybe they don't want me back!"

"I don't know. Chief Mathers seemed pretty excited about your application. I think your chances are pretty strong."

"Really?" he asked, sounding a little too excited.

"Yeah! And now I better figure out how to replace you, shouldn't I?"

"Not necessarily."

"I don't know if I can replace you," she teased.

"Oh trust me, Beth is going to be just great at this," Charles said. "Her training has been going very well. Yesterday, she sold six cases!"

Avery had taken on some trainees, placed in Charles' care. She had a new tasting area opening up next to a newly built pond. And she was trying to provide the staff to run it. But now it seemed she needed to hire more.

"I'll need three people to do what you do," Avery sighed.

Charles laughed loudly. "Don't worry...every week Beth has another friend interested in the job. You'll be just fine."

Avery crawled under the covers and made herself comfortable against a large stack of pillows. She'd never been so happy to be in bed before.

"Besides, I haven't said I'm leaving yet," Charles said.

Soon after, their conversation concluded, leaving Avery feeling unsettled. As she lay in bed, struggling to drift off to sleep, a realization dawned on her: her concern about finding a replacement for him wasn't as significant as she had initially thought. Avery cherished the ability to walk into the wine room and spend time with him whenever she wanted or needed to. Avery enjoyed having him around, and if he took another job, she would see him far less often.

That was what was really bothering her. The fact that it bothered her, irritated her. She closed her eyes and willed herself to sleep before she thought of anything else frustrating. It took her way too long, but by the time she fell asleep, Sprinkles had already been snoring loudly for a few hours.

It was the next night and Avery had just sat down at the table to have dinner with her parents when her father was ready to question her about the events of the previous night.

"So what exactly happened?" he asked. "I mean, I hear you and your friends found William stuffed behind the cabinet!"

Avery had only just taken the first sip of her shiraz.

"So, that's his name," Avery mumbled. "Did you know him?"

"William Gadling," he continued. "Of course, I knew him. He's the son of my old friend Patricia. Rest her soul."

Avery's mother placed the food on the table and shot her father an angry look.

"How can you talk about such things over dinner?" she asked.

"She writes about it!" her father argued.

He was referring to the few crime novels Avery had written and the very many crime novels that her late husband had written.

"It's alright, Mom," Avery said. "Besides, it really isn't all that interesting."

"Oh, there's no way it isn't interesting," her father laughed. "How can a murder be uninteresting?"

"I just mean that there isn't so much drama," Avery shrugged. "I was looking for my lip balm when I accidentally found him."

"On Marcus' farm," her father explained to her mother.

"You know Marcus?" Avery asked.

"Of course!" her mother answered. "We met many years ago."

"I see," Avery said, wondering why they hadn't been introduced sooner then.

"So, who is William then?" Avery asked. "I've never even heard his name."

Her mother huffed with frustration at the conversation being allowed to continue.

"Well, Patricia was one of our friend's neighbors." her father answered, not quite grasping the nature of her question. "We knew him when he was much younger, but she was always very proud of him."

"He could have become a drug dealer, and she would have been proud of him," her mother mumbled. "After her husband died, William was all she had, and so in her eyes, he could do no wrong. I used to get so tired of listening to her talk about him."

"You used to talk about Avery just as much. And I'm sure our friends were just as sick of it."

"Nonsense," her mother responded, winking at her.

"So, tell me about William," Avery tried again. "What did he do and stuff?"

"He never really struck a chord with me," her mother replied. "From the start, I had a gut feeling that he was trouble. It was just a hunch, you know? And I did mention it to you, didn't I? I had my suspicions all along."

Her father shrugged. "If you did, I didn't hear it."

"I said it," her mother sang. "He was always such an odd kid. It's a pity what's happened to him. I bet it was a case gone wrong."

"A case gone wrong?" Avery asked, reaching for her wine.

"He's a lawyer," her father finally said. "A good one at that."

"Good at winning cases, perhaps," her mother argued. "But not a good man in any way."

"What do you mean by that?" Avery asked.

Her mother swallowed hard and stared at her for a moment. Then, she waved her fork in her father's direction. "You tell her," she said.

Avery's father struggled not to roll his eyes. "He got himself into a bit of trouble in the community," he explained. "Some bad publicity, let's say."

"That's not unusual for a lawyer," Avery shrugged. "They have to take on cases that people disapprove of. It's part of the job."

"What he did was not part of the job," her father laughed.

"No," her mother agreed. "What he did was just downright awful."

"Then tell me!" Avery begged.

"He divorced a local couple, and the divorce was ugly and messy," her father explained. "It was the divorce between...what are their names again?"

"Katrina and Paul," her mother reminded him. "The Jones."

"Ah, yes," her father said. "Anyway, William helped Katrina take almost everything that Paul had. It was terrible for him. She took the house, half his money, the children, the cars...everything!"

"There were rumors he'd created evidence against Paul that wasn't true," her mother added.

"That's just speculation," her father argued. "We can't get too hung up on that."

Her father paused to take a monster-sized bite of his food. Just like with anything that he did, it irked her mother, who shot him a glare.

"Anyway," her father continued, still swallowing his bite. "A few months after the divorce, William and Katrina were hitched! It was quite the scandal."

"He married his client?" Avery asked.

"Yes!" her mother cried. "Can you imagine it?"

"It certainly seems a little strange," Avery said. "Do you think they fell in love while he was helping her divorce her husband?"

"That's what all the papers said," her father said. "Some of them even said they were together *before* the divorce happened."

Her mother crossed her arms and leaned back in her seat. "He shouldn't be allowed to keep practicing," she said.

"Well, he certainly isn't practicing anymore!" her father laughed.

Avery's mother gasped and softly slapped her father against his shoulder. "It's not funny!" she scolded him.

"What I can't believe is that he continued to be such a popular lawyer," her father continued, unfazed by her upset. "He always had a full client load and two separate assistants!"

"His career should have ended after that nonsense with Katrina. I mean, he moved into the house that Paul paid for! And drove his car!" her mother said.

Avery had to agree. It wasn't a kind thing to do. It didn't seem like a way in which a lawyer should behave.

"He's popular because he hardly ever loses a case," her father said. "He did a fantastic job of being a lawyer. That's why people paid him such good money."

The argument between her mother and father about what did and didn't make a good lawyer continued for the rest of the dinner. No matter how many times Avery tried to change the subject, they discussed William's morals for the entire night.

Chapter Four

Avery had dreamed all night about Paul taking William's life. She had no idea what Paul looked like, but her subconscious mind had simply shown her only what was below his head.

She didn't know how William had been murdered, so even that was vague. But she knew the subject matter of her dream well enough to feel completely unsettled when she woke up.

Despite there not being enough room on the bed for him, Sprinkles had curled up next to her. She struggled to move his heavy weight aside so she could get up and get dressed and find a way to distract herself from her thoughts.

By the time she'd poured herself a second cup of coffee, she still couldn't shake it from her mind. So, she reached for her phone and called Chief Mathers, hoping it would help.

"Avery!" he greeted cheerfully. "What a pleasant occasion to get a call from you so early in the morning."

"Sorry to disturb you on a Sunday," she said. "But there's something on my mind that I want to tell you."

"Go ahead," he answered. "And you're welcome to call me anytime you like."

"Thank you. It's about William's murder," she said. "I was with my parents last night, and they were talking to me about him. I know you've probably already thought of this, but I can't sleep unless I talk to you about it."

"Okay," he said uneasily. "Is everything alright?"

"Yes," she answered. "I heard about his case, where he married his client after settling her divorce. I just think it makes her ex-husband, Paul, a good suspect in all of this."

Chief Mathers chuckled. "Already ahead of you," he said. "And you're absolutely right. He's been on my suspect list since we arrived at the scene. He's been pretty public about his hatred toward William. You're a smart woman for seeing that, Avery."

"Thanks; sorry to have wasted your time," she responded.

"It was no waste at all," he said. "How are you doing after everything?"

"Oh, you know, I'm having nightmares and the usual," she laughed. "I suppose that's expected after something like that."

"It would be weird if you weren't having nightmares," Chief Mathers said. "Listen, if you need to talk about it, feel free to contact me. You know I always have time for you."

"Thanks," Avery said. "I think that's for it now, though. Have a good day, Chief!"

The call ended, and Avery sat down on the couch. She stared at the shelf of movies and didn't feel like watching any of them. She glanced over at the shelf of books and didn't find that inviting, either.

Avery didn't know what to do for the day. Although she felt better for having told Chief Mathers what she thought, it frustrated her that she thought that way at all. It had been her new goal to try to relax, and she was slowly learning that it was almost impossible.

She sighed and looked out the window. The weather was pleasant. Avery walked to the door and opened it, calling for Sprinkles to follow her. With her cup of coffee in hand, she walked toward the center of the vineyard where the new pond had been built.

The sun was warming the vines, and the breeze was blowing softly. Sprinkles was merrily trotting along, sniffing all the same plants he sniffed every time they walked that path.

The pond was still against the morning horizon, and Avery smiled proudly when she saw it. Many months of work had gone into that space, and it was finally complete. All that still needed to happen was for the party to start.

Around the pond was a large stretch of lawn with dainty tables and chairs sprawled out. Strings of lights had been installed by hand over the chairs, and at night it had a completely romantic look.

On one side, there was a bar that would soon be stocked with the best wine Le Blanc Cellars offered. Avery stared at the space and imagined the people and tourists of Los Robles laughing and drinking there.

She couldn't wait for that day. Beneath a small patch of trees was a small stage where she intended to have live bands play for special occasions.

Soon it would be operational, and despite the small fear that it would fail, she felt nothing but excitement for that time. Charles was meant to manage the space, though.

She thought about what the vineyard would be like without him. Her feelings about his application to rejoin the force were conflicting enough to cause a knot in her stomach. Despite her best wishes, nobody could tell her which of her feelings was the right one.

Avery loved what Charles meant to her business, but he was, most importantly, a good friend of hers. So, it meant that she only wanted what was best for him. She wanted to see him be happy. But she was learning that his happiness potentially meant that she had to lose him at the vineyard. It was impossible for her to decide which of her feelings toward it was the strongest.

Avery sat down on a small bench and contemplated what she might do to distract herself. In her attempt to relax, she had hired multiple members of staff to take some of the workload off her desk. The downside of that was that she could no longer use her work to distract her from the things that bothered her mind. Avery needed to find a new way to do that, and she had no idea where to begin.

Her eyes lost their focus on the view, and her mind ran away from her completely. She thought of everything all at once, creating a loud noise in her head that threatened to ruin her day.

It was only the ringing of her phone that pulled her back to Earth. By the time she realized her phone was ringing, it was one ring away from being dropped.

"Hello," she answered without checking who it was.

"What are you up to?" Tiffany's familiar voice greeted her.

"I'm sitting at the pond, and Sprinkles is rolling in the grass, making his fur green," Avery said, realizing she had left Sprinkles unwatched for far too long.

"Well, I've been gifted two tickets for free entrance into the Los Robles Zoo," Tiffany said. "They were given to me months ago, and I just realized they expire today. Would you like to go with me?"

Avery's prayers had been answered, and a worthy distraction had fallen directly into her lap.

"That sounds like a fantastic idea!" Avery said eagerly.

"Great, I'll pick you up in an hour," Tiffany said.

The zoo was busy that day. The weather was pleasant, and parents dragged their children down all the paths as they snapped endless photographs. Avery had never been to the zoo. It was much larger than it seemed from the outside.

She was pleased to know that they would likely be there for

many hours and that her distraction could not only see her through most of the day but would likely tire her out enough to sleep well that night.

It wasn't long before Avery and Tiffany had hot cups of coffee in hand as they made their way through the maze-like pathways.

After nearly two hours, they made it to an indoor space of the zoo. The walls were decorated with various patterns and bright colors, and at the end of the room was a large enclosure with a crowd of children standing around.

Avery stared through the glass but couldn't see anything particularly interesting. All she could see were some branches with green leaves at the end of them.

"Look," one of the kids said. "It's on that second branch there! I just saw it move!"

Avery searched the second branch eagerly, and finally, she saw the slightest hint of movement.

"What do you know?" Tiffany laughed. "Chameleons are pretty cool!"

"This one in particular," a man said to Avery's left.

He was a tall man with a monkey on his shoulder. The monkey seemed to be intently scrolling through some photographs on a cellphone.

"My name is Mr. Lupo," the man said. "I'm the owner of this zoo. And this is Alfonso."

The monkey, at the sound of its name, lifted its head and flashed them a garish smile.

"It's good to meet you! I'm Tiffany, and this is Avery," Tiffany said with a friendly smile.

"That's Tie-Dye," Mr. Lupo said, pointing to the chameleon. "He has quite a story, you know."

"I love a good story," Tiffany said eagerly.

"Well, it is quite a story for another day, perhaps," Mr. Lupo said, wasting no time. "But it was very stressful, and the police needed to get involved."

Both Avery and Tiffany gasped. "That sounds like quite the story!" Avery asked.

"Yes, this little guy was the center of an extensive investigation," Mr. Lupo laughed. "I don't think we ever would have solved it if we hadn't had such a skilled detective to help us."

"I'm glad he was found," Avery said with a smile.

"It wasn't the most important case in the world," Mr. Lupo continued. "But the man who helped us treated it as if it was. I think that made all the difference, despite the added complexity of involving another zoo. He somehow made quick work of it."

"I didn't know there was another zoo in Los Robles," Avery said.

"There isn't," Mr. Lupo said. "There was going to be one. But after the public learned about their theft of Tie-Dye here, it was boycotted."

Avery couldn't hide her smirk. She glanced back toward the chameleon and found that she felt sorry for the ordeal that it had been through. It seemed like such a silly thing for someone to do.

Avery glanced at the plaque on the side of the enclosure and confirmed that Tie-Dye was, in fact, the name of the chameleon.

"Good job, Tie-Dye!" Tiffany shouted.

Mr. Lupo laughed. "No, no," he said. "Good job, Charles! He was the detective on the case. He will have free entrance to this zoo for as long as he lives. If it wasn't for him, we might have closed."

Avery couldn't believe it. In a town as small as Los Robles, the chance of there being multiple detectives named Charles seemed unlikely. Still, she didn't think it was appropriate to ask Mr. Lupo if it was the same Charles she knew.

Still, at that moment, she felt selfish for ever thinking of how her vineyard would be affected if he rejoined the force. Detectives like Charles saved people and animals from unpleasant situations.

As a detective, he had changed lives and saved lives, and he could have continued to do so in their community. None of that would occur if he worked at the vineyard. He was a good detective, and the community could benefit from it more.

But then another thought plagued her mind.

What if something happens to him?

It had only occurred to her at that moment, as she imagined the gangsters that had taken Tie-Dye, that he could be in danger if he rejoined the force. Her heart couldn't handle it if something happened to him.

She'd experienced so much loss already. At least at Le Blanc Cellars, the risk of injury or death was low. As a detective, he would face dangerous criminals all the time. It was a stressful thought.

Even though she spent the rest of the day at the zoo, she couldn't get herself to relax again. It was no use.

By the time she got home, she was so worked up about it she could barely eat. She climbed into bed and stared at the ceiling all night.

Chapter Five

It was earlier than usual when Avery entered the wine room, her third cup of coffee in hand. Charles greeted her cheerfully.

"Morning," he sang. "It's good to see you first thing in the morning!"

"Morning, Charles," she said with a giggle. "I'm picking up some wine to take to Meat and Greet. They're thinking of stocking some of our reds."

"That's that new restaurant over there on the main stretch?" he asked.

"It is, indeed," she answered. "I knew the owner back when I was in school—Aaron. I never really liked him, but he's had a few successful businesses, and sales are always welcome."

Charles smiled as she passed him and went into the storeroom.

"You rarely do deliveries yourself," Charles said.

"No, that's right," Avery said between yawns. "But I wanted to invite him to the party, so I thought I would give him the invitation while I'm there."

Charles helped her with the various boxes of red wine as they loaded it into her car.

It was a beautiful day in Los Robles. The sun was shining, and the town seemed to be bustling with life and excitement for the tourist season. Avery was tired, though. A feeling that she hoped would pass soon enough. There was lots to do, and she was eager to do it.

"You know, I went to the zoo yesterday," Avery said. "It was my first time there!"

"Yeah?" he answered. "I've been there once too, but I've always been meaning to go back."

Avery chuckled. "You won't believe who I met," she said. "I met Mr. Lupo and Alfonso and the very famous chameleon, Tie-Dye."

The corners of Charles' mouth curled upward into a bright smile. "How are they all doing?" he asked. "Tie-Dye is the mascot for that zoo!"

"Well, they told me what happened with the chameleon. Mr. Lupo spoke very highly of you."

"He mentioned me?" Charles said.

Avery was pleased. She had suspected Mr. Lupo had been referring to *her* Charles. But now she had confirmed it. Which only solidified her conflicted feelings about the whole matter.

"That was my last case," Charles said. "After that, I left the force and came here. I've had a much more peaceful life since then."

"There's nothing more pleasant than wine, is there?" Avery teased.

"You're right," Charles said.

"Listen, I think that if you want to rejoin the force, you absolutely should," she said. "Los Robles could use a good detective, and clearly you are one."

"Thank you," Charles said. "But I'm still confused about

what I might do. Like I said, it's peaceful here. A police precinct is the furthest thing from peaceful."

"I suppose that's true, isn't it?" she said. "At least you know you can visit here any time you like and any time you need a quiet moment."

He seemed happy with that response.

"Well, I better go and deliver this. I need to be back here in an hour to receive the delivery of glasses for the new tasting area."

"I'll leave you to it, then."

Avery closed the trunk and drove away from her farm. She didn't like to leave it. She understood the peacefulness Charles was talking about. In her rearview mirror, her home grew smaller.

It was a comforting thought that she missed her home whenever she was away from it. It was nice to feel that way. She hadn't felt that way when she had first moved away from the city to the farm.

At that time, she felt that she would never love a home as much as she'd loved the home she'd shared with her husband. But the more she healed from it, the more she loved her new home at the vineyard.

It had a lot to do with her friends.

She was eager to deliver the wine and get back to the vineyard as fast as possible. Thankfully, the drive was beautiful. As she drove, her mind wandered, and she thought about the zoo, the chameleon, and the strangeness of that crime. That reminded her of the gangsters that had stolen Tie-Dye, and somehow, it led her mind to thoughts of William.

She knew his parents had passed away, but his wife was still very much alive, and she pitied any family that had to go through loss. Avery knew how difficult it was, and how quickly love could change.

As her heart saddened at the thought of it, she pulled into the parking lot of Meat and Greet.

Inside, the restaurant was busy. It was a new restaurant, and everyone in Los Robles was eager to taste their menu. Avery had seen the reviews, and they'd all been positive. She was eager to know that her wine would accompany the five-star food.

She found a server to help her, and out of the corner of her eye, she noticed Aaron seated at a nearby table. He was deep in conversation with a friend of his, and she was happy about that.

His conversations had always been boring to her, and she didn't want to get roped into one. However, she couldn't help but turn her ear to him when she heard him speak William's name. Avery wasn't sure why she was so intrigued by it. Perhaps it was because she had seen his dead body.

She might have expected not to want to hear about him at all, but instead, she found herself desperate for any piece of information she could get about him and his life.

"It sounds terrible," Aaron said. "But I got lucky when William died, I tell you."

His friend laughed, even though the statement sounded nothing like a joke.

"No, seriously!" Aaron continued. "You have no idea. His death has saved me a huge amount of money!"

"What do you mean?" his friend asked.

"Well, he came in here one day, and it was clear that he was in a bad mood," Aaron explained. "He ordered our flaming steak dinner. As you know, the steak is set on fire when it is served. It's kind of fun and showy."

"Yeah, I ate that the first time I was here. It was quite the experience," his friend added.

"Right, well, William ordered it and all went according to plan and the steak was set on fire. The table cheered and gawked at the show. Then, he took a bite of it!" Aaron explained. He paused to take a sip of his coffee and leaned back in his seat.

"Needless to say, he burned his mouth. And I'll be honest, he burned it quite badly. I mean, the meat had been on fire only a few moments before."

"I can imagine it must have been rather hot," his friend said.

"Precisely," Aaron continued. "Anyway, he said nothing to me. A few days later, I'm informed that I am being sued by William Gadling. He claimed that because of the burns, he could not speak properly and that because of that he'd lost an important case."

"You have to be kidding me," the friend commented.

Avery had to agree with him. It did sound absolutely insane to her that he would have done something like that. But it wasn't entirely unheard of. It just wasn't the kind of thing people in the Los Robles community were known for.

"Surely he didn't win, though," the friend said.

"Of course, he won!" Aaron said. "He's an excellent lawyer, and he had a good case against me. I didn't know what to do, and I had a terrible lawyer. So, I owed him a lot of money. It was a ridiculous time of my life."

"I can imagine," his friend said, unhelpfully. "And now that he's dead, you don't owe him the money?"

"Nope. I was worried that I'd have to pay it to his next of kin," Aaron said. "But he clearly wasn't expecting to die, and no such clause was ever added."

"Good heavens," his friend commented, which was precisely what Avery was thinking.

"It would have cost me my business," Aaron said. "I'm so scared of it now that I'm considering removing the item from the menu completely. It only takes one case like this to give everyone the same idea. I wake up every day afraid that someone might sue me for something."

Avery couldn't pretend to be busy any longer and left the building. She sat in the car in silence for a while. The more she learned about William, the worse of a person he seemed to be.

Chapter Six

As Avery made the drive home, she couldn't stop thinking about the fact that Aaron had a good motive to take William's life. But she didn't want to jump to conclusions until she knew the story was true. In school, Aaron had always been the one to spread rumors, so she couldn't automatically trust any word out of his mouth.

If she was going to tell Chief Mathers about a potential new suspect, she had to be sure about it.

As Avery drove onto the road leading to her house, she felt peace creep back into her heart. She was happy to be home and grateful that the delivery hadn't taken too long.

Sprinkles ran to greet her as she got home, his tail wagging as he ran. As usual, he wouldn't let her take another step before she patted him on the head and gave him multiple kisses.

When she was allowed into the house, she poured herself a cup of tea. Her hands were shaking from too much coffee already, and it was too early for a glass of wine. It was time for her to catch up with admin work, but as she did so, she found herself distracted by the story she'd heard Aaron tell.

Eventually, she found herself staring at a half-written

sentence, and she couldn't remember what she was trying to write. All she could think of was the insane fact that William had sued the Meat and Greet restaurant for burning his mouth on the food.

She couldn't let it go and needed to know more. So, she opened her browser and searched for any information on the case. Multiple articles came up in her search. There, she saw images of a proud-looking William as he was interviewed after the case. As she read through the articles, it became clear that the case had boosted his popularity as a lawyer and, after that, he was getting clients like never before. It was sickening to Avery, but she understood it, too.

From what she could understand, nobody had expected him to win. When the case had started, the odds had been against him. William had represented himself and had won the case with ease by using various loopholes in the system.

The case had made national news, and he had been interviewed multiple times for television. It made her feel bad for Aaron. There were a few articles where Aaron had been given the opportunity to speak. In those, he looked tired, stressed, and at his wit's end.

She watched some of the videos but found them uncomfortable to watch. Partly, it was because she didn't agree with what William had done. But mostly, it was because she had only ever seen him after death. His dead, unfeeling eyes had been the only way she'd known William. It was odd to see him animated and to hear his voice.

Then, she moved on to reading some of the articles. Some of them had a positive view of the case. They were in William's favor and spoke only good words about him. Other articles took a negative approach to the case.

Some people agreed with Avery. They saw William as someone who had taken a chance to make money and made a strong attempt to save his career after having married one of his clients. So, she looked up any articles with Paul and Katrina included—the names of the married couple he had separated.

That led her to search for articles about their wedding. There were many, and all of them were negative. They spoke about how he had hurt Paul, and most of the articles had been focused on Paul. Some of them had even been written by Paul. There were interviews in which Paul spoke about his heartbreak and how shocked he had been to learn about their marriage and relationship.

There was one interview where William and Katrina spoke about how they had accidentally found love and how they hadn't intended for things to go that way. The answers they gave seemed rehearsed and well thought-through. As much as they answered the questions, they provided little information. It seemed as if they had agreed to do the interview in order to stop the articles from being written.

One thing stood out to Avery most: neither seemed to show any remorse for what they had done to Paul. All she saw was a happy couple who looked as if they had won the lottery.

As she went through more articles about William, she learned that there had been multiple cases against him, too. From what she could tell, he had hurt many people in his career.

There were cases in which he had helped clients sue people for minor offenses, much like he had done to Meat and Greet. There were other cases in which he had done borderline unlawful things to get himself the win.

In short, he was a scumbag, and the more she read about him, the more she believed that to be true. It seemed wrong to think about a dead person so negatively, but she couldn't help it. Avery was putting herself in the shoes of his victims and understood their hatred toward him.

There was something Avery had noticed about the cases. All the cases against him had been thrown out, mostly because of clerical errors and missing evidence. Others were pulled with little explanation. It left a nasty taste in Avery's mouth, but she couldn't help reading further. Most of what she was reading, she didn't like.

The more images she saw of him smiling proudly, the more she thought he looked smug and condescending.

Some of the videos and articles had a space for people to leave comments. Avery could tell from those that there were many people who felt the same way she felt about William.

Then, she searched for articles about his death. There weren't many yet, but most of them were lengthy. As far as she could tell, the police hadn't revealed a lot yet. Most of what people knew was that he was dead and that it was under suspicious circumstances.

There was an interview in which Marcus had been asked to talk about the ordeal. Avery watched it and felt some pride when she saw Marcus answering the questions politely and with taste. At last, it felt as if the person being interviewed showed some empathy.

There were some articles in which the family had said a few words, and most of them said that he would be missed. None of it seemed particularly personal, and most of it seemed like something one might read on a card.

Avery wondered if perhaps he hadn't been popular even among his own family members. She couldn't be certain, though.

The statement by the police regarding the murder was brief. They simply mentioned that a body was found and identified as William. Avery could almost hear Chief Mathers' voice in her head as she read it.

Then she scrolled down to the comments again. What she read made her uneasy. There were typical comments sending condolences to the family. But there were also comments by people who said that they weren't surprised he'd been murdered.

It appeared that William had many enemies, and many

people hated him. Those people appeared to be pretty vocal about it too.

She could think of two people who hated him that she knew of. Both Aaron and Paul were outspoken about how they felt about him, and Aaron had even gone as far as to say he was lucky that William had died.

Her mind was consumed with thoughts and speculation, and she wasn't sure who was best to talk to about it. She wanted to phone Chief Mathers, but she didn't want to assume, again, that he hadn't already looked into it.

It wasn't her job to solve the murder. Only, she couldn't get it out of her mind, no matter what she did.

She was so deep in thought that when her phone rang, it gave her such a fright she almost fell out of her chair. "Hello," she answered without looking at the contact name.

Her heart was pounding in her chest, and she was out of breath from fright.

"Hello, ma'am, we're here to deliver your glasses," a friendly voice said on the other end of the line.

"Oh, thank goodness," she replied before hanging up.

Sprinkles walked happily at her side as she made her way up the driveway to meet the delivery driver. She signed the papers, happy for the distraction from her dark thoughts, and showed them to the storeroom where hundreds of new wine glasses, branded with the vineyard's name, were packed and ready for use.

When they were done, Avery peered back at her house and knew that if she walked back in there, she would go straight back to her laptop and get consumed by the mystery of William again.

Instead, she rushed into the kitchen, opened a chilled bottle of champagne, and raced out of the house before she gave in to temptation again. Sprinkles bounced along with her.

Avery checked the time. It was almost time for Charles to end his day, so she took two of the new glasses and made her way down toward the pond. It was still a few hours until sunset, but soft clouds had dotted across the skies, making for a wonderful view.

She nestled herself into one of the new chairs on the lawn and phoned Charles.

"Don't tell me you've left yet," she said when he answered.

"I was about to," he answered. "Why? What's wrong?"

"Nothing's wrong, but I was wondering if you'd join me for a glass of bubbles at the pond," she said. "The glasses have arrived, and I'm taking one for a test drive."

"That sounds fantastic; I'll see you soon," he answered.

Avery filled the glasses and waited happily for Charles as she watched the clouds move over her head. It was a wonderful space on the farm. There was open air above her, in between some thick trees and vines. It felt like a little opening in a sacred space. The pond had a fountain in the center, and the sound of running water was enough to drown out any bad thoughts. She'd liked the little clearing for as long as she could remember.

When she had been a child and her parents had been busy running the farm, she would often go out to that spot and build forts out of sticks and sheets and spend full days there.

"Nice spot you have here," Charles teased.

"Thank you," Avery said, handing him a glass as he took a seat.

"Thank you for the invite. I was just wondering what I was going to do today after work. I'd hit a blank, but thankfully, you answered that question for me."

"I figured we could share the first glass of wine to be sipped at the new, finally completed tasting area," Avery said with a bright smile.

"Well, I think it deserves a toast, don't you?" he answered.

Avery raised her glass, and so did Charles. At that moment, she remembered her favorite toast, one that she hadn't used in years, and one that seemed fitting for the day.

"Champagne for my real friends, real pain for my sham friends!" she toasted happily.

"I couldn't have said it better myself!" Charles said, tapping his glass against hers.

The chilled bubbles tickled her throat as they celebrated a space that had taken most of her time for months to pull together.

Soon, it wouldn't be quite as quiet as it was at that moment. There would be people drinking and laughing as live music filtered through the air. There would be people with trays carrying glasses to tables. Hopefully, one day they'd have lavish parties.

"You're a good friend," Charles said, breaking the moment of silence. "Thank you for what you said to me today. I still haven't made a decision, but it was nice to hear that you support me in this."

"Of course," Avery said. "We care about each other. And that care extends outside of what you mean to me as an employee."

Charles and Avery spent the time sipping champagne until the sun had turned the sky bright orange and Sprinkles had thrown himself into the pond.

Chapter Seven

Charles walked Avery and a soaked Sprinkles back toward her house. The champagne bottle was empty, and both glasses were tucked into the fingers of one hand. By the time they made it to the house, the sun had completely set, and it was dark outside.

"What about a cup of coffee?" Avery offered.

"I won't say no to that," Charles said happily.

Avery unlocked the door, and Charles took his usual seat at her kitchen table. He was quiet as she prepared the coffee—quieter than he usually was.

She wanted to ask him about it, but she knew him well enough to know that if she just waited long enough, he would eventually tell her what was bothering him.

"Have you eaten today?" Avery asked.

"No," Charles said. "I was going to eat lunch, but I just forgot."

"I have some leftovers I could heat up if you like?" she offered. "It will take only five minutes."

Charles happily accepted, and even then, his eyes were fixated on a spot on the table. He was deep in thought and remained that way until Avery placed the bowl of food on the table in front of him.

Avery made some small talk, which felt odd now that they had become such good friends.

"I need to ask you a favor," he eventually asked.

"Go ahead," Avery said with a smile.

"I need a few days off," he said bluntly.

"How many days? And when?"

It wasn't ever a problem when Charles needed time off. He hardly ever requested it, and when he did, it was almost always at a convenient time.

"I'm going to need a day or two every week for the next few weeks," he said with a frown.

That was not convenient at all. Still, it was curious, and Avery couldn't help but wonder what he would be doing on those days.

"Why?" she blurted out.

Charles sighed. "Mathers has made me an offer that I think I must take. He's asked me to join them on the Gadling case, and then I would know if I was ready to rejoin the force or not," he explained.

He paused for a moment to take a bite of his food. "I wasn't going to do it. But the more I think about it, the more it makes sense to me."

"I suppose that does make some kind of sense," she said. "When did he say this to you?"

"A few days ago," Charles said. "I've been thinking about it almost constantly since he asked. But, surely, if I didn't want to do it, then I wouldn't still be thinking about it, right?"

"Yeah, I guess so," Avery said. "It's not a bad idea at all. If you take the case and hate it, then you know you shouldn't go back. But..."

"If I take the case and love it," Charles finished for her. "Then I guess the decision is made."

"Yeah."

Avery could see the anguish in his eyes as he struggled to make a decision. She didn't blame him for struggling. It was a big decision to make.

"You can have the days off," she relented.

It wasn't the greatest time for him to do so. There was still so much to prepare for the party, and she simply enjoyed having him around. But she was eager for him to make up his mind about it all, and this would speed it up.

"Besides, it will give Beth a chance to prove herself, too. I'll leave the training of the newbies in your hands, still," Avery said. "And I'll still need your help with the party."

"Of course," Charles said.

It always felt strange to Avery when she needed to speak to Charles as if he was an employee. Especially since she knew he was one and that she should speak like that with him. But she preferred speaking to him like a friend.

"Are you nervous about taking on a case?" Avery asked, dropping the boss stuff.

"I honestly haven't even thought about that yet," Charles said. "I guess I'll know when I spend my first day back at the station."

"Chief Mathers will be excited to hear about your decision," she said with a smile.

"He's been nagging me about it for days," Charles said. "He's struggling with the case, it seems."

"I think it is exciting," Avery said with wide eyes. "So, what will you do first?"

"Mathers wants me to re-interview Paul. He's William's wife's ex-husband," Charles said with a puzzled expression.

"Yeah, I know," Avery laughed. "My parents told me all about the scandal of William marrying his client. I was reading all the articles about it this morning."

"All of them?" Charles asked, looking up at her.

"Yeah, well, as many of them as I could," she said. "You should watch the interviews. Paul was furious at them."

"Well, Mathers seems to think I might be able to get some more information out of him. I'm not so sure, though," Charles said.

"I think you're going to do well!" Avery cheered. "Mr. Lupo would agree with me if he was here right now."

"Does he still have that monkey on his shoulder?" Charles asked.

Avery laughed. "Alfonso? Yeah!"

"Odd man," Charles muttered. "Anyway, I better go. I'm going to have to let Mathers know about my decision, and he'll likely want me to get to it as soon as possible. Is it okay if I take the first day off tomorrow?"

"Yeah, yeah," Avery agreed with a wave of her hand.

They bid farewell to each other like friends, and she watched and waved as he left. It was still early, despite the darkness outside. She didn't know what else to do, so she took her laptop and crawled into bed with it, ready to learn all she could about Paul.

Avery was reading as much as she could about those involved in the case, but she wasn't sure she was really taking any of it in. The night was chilly, and she was comfortable. Her eyes were starting to burn when she felt her phone buzz on the bed next to her.

It had been such a quiet night that she jumped at the sound and feel of it, clutching her chest as she caught her breath. It was a message from Charles that had startled her.

Chief says you can watch the interrogation if you want. In case you'd like to write another book. Says it can be like the others.

Avery looked over to her dresser where a heap of her latest

book sat, untouched and unsold. She hadn't written many books. Those she had written had followed in her late husband's footsteps. Only, hers had been based on actual crimes in Los Robles, whereas her husband's books were entirely made up.

She liked to see the books with her name on the spines, but she did not enjoy the process of writing them. Avery had been too involved in the cases as she prepared to write the books, and that involvement had taken a toll on her. So, she knew what her response would be.

No, thank you. I'll sit this one out.

She remembered how she had felt after the last book had been released. As proud as she'd been of the final product, she was afraid every night when she went to bed. All that she had learned about murderers and how unsuspecting they could be had made her completely paranoid. She had watched multiple interrogations in preparation for her last book, and all of them had left her feeling uncomfortable.

When the book had been released, there had been reports of unhappy members of the town who had felt she had been allowed to see too much. It had never been her intention to profit off of the death of another human being, but some people had seen it that way.

It left a foul taste in her mouth. As she stared at the pile of books, she wondered if her husband had ever felt the same. If he had, he had never said so. Besides, the murders in his books had not been based on true stories like hers had.

She'd done her best to change enough of the story to make it new. But those who'd been affected by the murders that inspired those stories had still seen too many similarities. For a while, it had made her unpopular.

Avery sighed and looked away from the books, making a mental note to put them away the next day. She didn't want to look at them again; she didn't want the reminder. Although, she knew that soon those feelings of apprehension would dissipate, and she'd go back to feeling proud of her book.

In reality, here was much to be proud of. Apart from a few complaints, the book had done remarkably well. It made her wonder if she'd ever write another book. She hoped she would, but every time that the thought crossed her mind, she found herself changing her thought subject.

Avery simply didn't want to be involved in such terrible stories again. Perhaps it was time for her to write about a different subject. As she turned her attention back to her laptop with the idea of searching for an alternative topic for her next book, she glanced down at the clock.

It was far later than she thought. Charles' message had clearly snapped her out of a moment of doomscrolling as it was almost midnight. She wanted to get some rest, and she didn't want to read more about those potentially involved in the murder.

It would most likely affect her dreams. Her mind had a habit of doing that, and it could be rather disturbing at times. So, she put her laptop aside and lay down to close her eyes. Avery hoped to simply drift to sleep, but, naturally, that wasn't going to happen.

She was restless, and it was because of Charles. As much as he was certain Beth could take over his position and do well, she didn't know how she would feel if he had to stop working there.

In her spirit, she also knew when he did the interrogation the next day there was a strong chance he would realize he missed the work, and he would go back. She knew the only reason he thought about staying at the vineyard was because of her.

Avery pressed her head to the pillow and did her best to slow her breathing. She needed to relax if she had any hope of getting sleep. It worked. Soon, she was fast asleep.

But just as expected, her dreams were not prepared to let her fully relax. In her dream, she found herself unable to move. Her back was pressed against something cold, and the front of her was pressed against something hard. She couldn't see well, but as she struggled, she saw a narrow beam of light ahead of her.

Her heart rate spiked as she realized she was trapped. She pushed with all her might against the hard surface that held her in place, and it would not budge. Then, she heard a sound.

It sounded like plastic rolling across the floor. She felt the object bump into her feet. Avery could not move her head, but she glanced down as far as she could. There it was...the lip balm that she'd dropped in the wine cave.

Her heart sank as she realized where she was. She was trapped between the cabinet and the wall. When she glanced up again, she was met by the sight of her own face screaming back at her.

Chapter Eight

Avery's head was pounding as she poured her first cup of coffee for the day. She hadn't slept well, and she was in no mood for the day that lay before her. It was her designated day to get through all her mind-numbing admin.

For a brief moment, she thought perhaps a mind-numbing task was just what her aching head needed. Then again, perhaps it would shut her brain off completely. It was a risk she would have to be willing to take.

She'd skipped admin day before, and it had not ended well for her. It had resulted in her being awake until midnight on her next admin day, slogging through all the tedious work. Unfortunately for her, there were some parts of the vineyard's operations that simply could not be handed over to someone else.

Most of it involved decision-making of some kind.

Avery slumped down in front of her laptop. The steam from her coffee filtered into the air as she searched desperately for her reading glasses. She hated that she needed them, but with her headache, she couldn't risk facing the screen without them.

When she did find them, she discovered she could barely see through them. They were completely filthy, and she couldn't for the life of her figure out what might have happened the last time she'd worn them. When she finally had them clean and opened up her laptop, she was faced with her search results from the night before.

Avery groaned, closing all the tabs. There was a risk of her going down the rabbit hole from which she knew she would never return. No, she had a task at hand and needed to stick to it. She opened up her email, and as usual, it took its time to load.

So, to pass that time she checked her phone for any messages from Charles. She knew he would be at the station already and was likely preparing to start his interrogation. But there was nothing from him yet.

There was, however, a message on the Stammtisch group. It was a wine-related joke that Avery had seen at least twenty times already. There was also a message from her mother. It was a link to a news article about the health risks of eating broccoli.

There was no way that Avery was going to open the link. She had received many of those from her mother, and any time she'd actually read them, they had only upset her.

Finally, her emails opened, and she saw one at the top from Aaron. He was thanking her for the delivery of the wine and had sent the proof of payment for it.

She was curious about him, as she still felt that he could be a suspect. Still, she didn't know enough to be certain, yet. So, she cooked up a last-minute plan. She phoned Tiffany.

"Hello!" Tiffany sang.

"Morning," Avery said. "What are you doing tonight?"

"Nothing much, why? What did you have in mind?"

"I'm trying to find out some more information on Aaron, the guy who owns that Meat and Greet restaurant," Avery explained.

"I've been meaning to go there. Wanna get some dinner tonight?" Tiffany asked.

"You're reading my mind!" Avery laughed.

"So, what's the deal with this Aaron guy?" Tiffany asked.

"I heard him talking about William the other day," Avery explained.

"William?"

"You know, the guy behind the cabinet," Avery sighed.

"Oh, I'm sure everyone is talking about that guy," Tiffany laughed. "This is a small town, you know."

"Well, this was different. He was saying stuff that could very well make him a suspect, but I want to be sure before I go to Chief Mathers about it," Avery explained.

Tiffany let out an excited giggle. "A stakeout?" she asked. "You really do know how to have fun!"

With that, they agreed they would meet for dinner. It was enough incentive for Avery to knuckle down and get her work done for the day. Sprinkles slept at her feet the entire day as she worked, and in the end, it didn't take her nearly as long as she thought it might.

By the time the end of the day came around, she still had heard nothing from Charles. Much to her disappointment.

The restaurant looked completely different at night than it did in the day. There were soft lights all around, and every table was filled with people. Quiet jazz filtered in and out of the space as waiters moved swiftly with meals and drinks around them.

The food was excellent. It had been a long time since Avery had eaten quite that well. The dishes were presented beautifully, and around them were many happy well-fed tables of people. The atmosphere felt almost electric. It was quickly becoming clear why the people of the village kept going back there and why all the reviews were excellent ones.

As a business owner, it made Avery feel a little competitive.

"Should I open a restaurant at the vineyard?" she asked, taking a bite of her steak.

Tiffany almost choked. "Do you not have enough going on there already?"

Avery shrugged. "Yeah, but I don't have one of these." She motioned to the space around them and smiled.

Tiffany had been in a good mood that night. She enjoyed working at the vineyard and having Avery as a boss. It had freed up a lot more time in her day, and she was looking healthy and well-rested.

Avery was happy to see her friend that way. She also liked having Tiffany's help at the vineyard.

"I have news," Tiffany said with a smirk. "And I'll tell you, but you have to promise you won't laugh at me."

"I can't promise that," Avery said, reaching for her glass of merlot. "But I am dying to know what you might say next.

"I've decided I am ready to date again," she announced.

At that moment, a looming figure approached their table and stopped.

"Well, isn't that the best news I've heard all evening," he said.

Both their heads shot up, and a smiling Aaron looked down at them. He had his most charming smile across his face as he nodded a greeting to Avery. Tiffany's cheeks turned a bright shade of pink as she sipped the last bit of merlot from her glass.

"Tiffany, this is Aaron. He owns the place."

Aaron gave a curt bow and held out his hand to shake hers.

"It's a pleasure to meet you," she giggled. "This is a beautiful restaurant."

Avery hadn't seen Tiffany giggle like that since they were in high school, and she knew she would tease her about it later. Her friend jumped easily into some small talk with the restaurant owner, but Avery had a hard time concentrating. She couldn't stop picturing him taking William's life.

Although he was a handsome man, Avery found it hard to

find him attractive. Her mind couldn't stop considering that he could be a criminal, a murderer. That thought made him significantly more ugly to her.

He was a tall man, with dark hair. Avery had never seen him in anything other than a suit. He was exactly Tiffany's type. He also had money.

"Is everything alright with your food, ladies?" he asked, eventually.

"Yes, of course," Avery answered, breaking her silence. "It's lovely; some of the best food in town!"

"That is excellent news," he said, reaching for the bottle of wine.

He refilled their glasses for them, calling over a nearby server. He ordered two desserts for them, on the house.

"Thank you for the wine," he said, turning his attention to Avery. "It's been a very popular addition to the menu. I fear we'll sell out quicker than I thought."

"Doesn't bother me!" Avery teased. "Order as much as you like. I'll send Tiffany to deliver."

Avery flashed Tiffany a knowing smile and watched as her cheeks turned pink again.

"Oh!" Aaron said excitedly. "In that case, you can expect my next order tomorrow."

It looked as if Tiffany wanted the Earth to swallow her in. Avery enjoyed teasing her. She always had for as long as they'd been friends. Tiffany shot her a glare, warning her to stop.

"Will you be attending the opening of our new tasting area, then?" Tiffany asked.

"New tasting area?" he asked, looking over at Avery.

Avery reached into her bag for the invitation she hadn't yet given him.

"I meant to give this to you the other day," she said. "But you were in a meeting or something."

She handed the invitation to him, and he immediately opened it. He read through the entire invitation.

"Oh, you must come," Tiffany said. "It is such a beautiful place, and it is going to be such a great party!"

"I'll certainly be there," he said with a smile. "But this is still some time away. And I would so like to see you again before that."

He was talking to Tiffany. She was so shocked that she almost spat out the sip of wine that she'd had in her mouth.

"S...sure," she said, flabbergasted.

"Excellent! It's a date, then!" he said.

Avery watched as they exchanged numbers, at which point Aaron finally left their table, and they finished their meal. Although she didn't have the space for it, Avery wolfed down the dessert that he had arranged for them.

"You realize you've just accepted a date with a man that I think might be guilty of murder, don't you?" Avery said.

Tiffany gasped. "I completely forgot about that!"

Avery burst out laughing. "That's why we were here in the first place!"

"You have to tell me, then. Why do you think he might have killed William?" Tiffany asked.

"Well, I overheard him talking about how William had sued him for a burned mouth. He had owed him huge amounts of money," Avery summarized.

"That was this place?" Tiffany said. "I heard about that!"

"Yeah! So, that sounds kind of like a motive to me," Avery said.

Tiffany sipped on her wine as if she'd been completely defeated. "You're right, it does."

"Well, we've learned nothing new here tonight," Avery said. "So, maybe you can learn something while you're on your date!"

"You're kidding," Tiffany said. "That is not the kind of stakeout that I signed up for."

"You accepted a date with him!" Avery said.

"I know," Tiffany sighed. "Fine, I'll see what I can find out on our date, but I'm not getting in a car with him."

"Smart decision," Avery said sarcastically. "Listen, at the very least, see what you can find out from him. Help me decide if he might be a suspect or not."

"You're kidding," Tiffany said. "Like I'm some kind of spy?"

"We got nothing tonight!" Avery said. "I still want to know."

"How do you suggest I do that?" Tiffany said. "How do you expect me to work the topic of the murder into the conversation?"

Avery thought about it for a moment. "I don't know," she said. "You obviously can't be outright with it."

"So I need to ask him in a way that makes it seem like I am not asking him?" Tiffany asked.

"Yes, exactly!" Avery cheered. "Brilliant idea!"

"And how am I supposed to do *that*?" Tiffany asked.

"You'll think of something!"

Tiffany sipped her wine nervously. "This is a bad idea."

"Okay, you don't *have* to do it," Avery said. "But it would be very helpful to me."

"Well, I kinda want to know if he's a murderer or not, too," Tiffany said. "He's very attractive. What if I discover he's also really nice and filthy rich? He'd be perfect for me and then I'll have fallen in love with a murderer! It would be highly disappointing."

Avery almost spat out her wine as she laughed. "Well, then you better think of something! Why don't you just ask him where he was that night or around that time?"

Tiffany stretched her eyes wide. "That's an excellent idea. That's a much easier way to do it."

Avery nodded. "If he has an alibi, then we can count him out, and the two of you can run away together," she teased. "If he has no alibi, then you can ditch him at the date and come right to me, and we'll tell the police what we know."

"And if he doesn't answer at all?" Tiffany asked. "What if I don't manage to work it into the conversation?"

"Then I hope you simply have a good time and get home safely," Avery said.

They finished their desserts and headed home. Before Avery went to sleep, she checked her phone for any news from Charles and found nothing. She was dying to know how his day had gone. She typed out a quick message to him.

So? How did it go?

She waited a few moments for a reply as she struggled to get herself comfortable. It was a silent night at the vineyard as she contemplated where she might put her new restaurant if she ever decided that she wanted one.

It was her favorite kind of daydream. Every one of her exciting changes to the vineyard had started just like that. She didn't know what she was going to do with her time once the new tasting area was up and running smoothly. All of her efforts had gone into that space, and that work was soon ending. Once the space was launched, there would be someone to take it over and run it on behalf of Avery.

She remembered what Tiffany had said about where she would find the time. She had felt that way about every new idea she'd had, and yet, she'd done it, anyway. Whether that was excitement or stubbornness, she didn't know.

Sprinkles let out a loud sigh as he drifted off to sleep. Avery checked one last time for news from Charles. Then, she closed her eyes and fell right to sleep, getting the rest that she had missed out on the night before.

Chapter Nine

Avery lay comfortably in her spot on the couch as she watched her favorite cooking show. The food looked so delicious, and it only increased her desire to have a restaurant at the vineyard.

It was something she didn't even know she had been missing. She wanted to make people feel the way she had when she was at dinner with Tiffany a few nights before. Avery had felt warm, happy, and well-fed. She had slept well that night because of it.

As she watched, she made notes of all the meals that seemed particularly delicious as she imagined a wonderful menu for her restaurant. Of course, she knew it would take a little more than just a menu, but she wanted the idea to flourish a little more.

Soon, her page was filled with a long list of food that she not only wanted for her dream restaurant, but she also wanted to taste them all that very minute. Instead, she went into the kitchen and warmed up some leftovers.

It was nothing special...just a simple chicken stew. But with every bite she took, she imagined she was eating what she was watching on the screen. It was a fun game to play. Sprinkles lay curled up at her feet, fast asleep.

Avery was about to write down yet another meal item on her fantasy menu when her phone rang. Without looking, she knew who it would be. It was the night that Tiffany had gone on her date with Aaron, and Avery had been dying to know about how it had gone.

"Finally, although, isn't it a little early for your date to have ended?" Avery said as she answered the phone.

She muted the television; she didn't want to concentrate on both, but she still wanted to see the food on the screen.

"Ugh," Tiffany groaned. "Normally, yes, but tonight I wish it had ended ages ago."

"That bad?" Avery laughed. "I want to know everything."

"There's just so little to tell!" Tiffany complained. "The entire thing was awfully boring. It felt as if we spoke constantly, but said nothing of interest at all. I don't think I've ever been on such a tedious date."

"Where did you go, then?" Avery asked, desperate for any kind of detail.

"You will not believe this," Tiffany said. "But he took me to his own restaurant."

"He did not."

"He did," she answered. "And he was pleased about it, he said, because he wouldn't have to pay the bill. In the end, I tipped the server. I felt bad!"

Avery burst out laughing. "You are kidding."

"I wish I was," Tiffany responded meagerly.

"I'm really sorry. That sounds kind of awful," Avery said with a chuckle.

"You know, this whole thing makes me wonder if I really am ready for dating," Tiffany said, sounding completely defeated. "I don't know if I can go through something like that again. There are so many better ways I could have spent that time."

"Surely you two had to have spoken about *something?*" Avery asked.

"Yes," her friend answered. "We talked about him. That was all he seemed to be interested in. And he isn't even all that interesting."

"Well, not all men are boring. Don't let this deter you," Avery responded, trying to be helpful.

"Speaking of dates," Tiffany said. "When are you going on your date with Charles?"

In the background of the call, Avery could hear the sounds of Tiffany pulling a cork from a bottle and reaching for a glass.

"I don't know," she said, topping up her own wine. "We haven't really discussed that yet."

"You're still going to do it, though?" her friend asked.

"Yeah," Avery said. "But I actually haven't heard from him in days. I'm not sure how long I'm supposed to wait until I get concerned."

"I wouldn't worry about that," Tiffany said. "If something had happened to Charles, you can be sure Deb would have told you about it already."

Avery laughed. Tiffany was right. There was nobody who knew information quicker than Deb and nobody who could spread it quicker, either.

"It feels weird to think about going on a date," Avery said. "But I try not to think about it too much."

"You'll be fine," Tiffany sighed. "It's not as if he's a stranger."

"I suppose."

"So, why do you think he's been so quiet?" Tiffany asked. "Do you think he's avoiding you?"

"No. He's been thinking about going back to the police force. It weighs heavily on him. I think he just needs some space to think."

"Oh, well, that makes sense."

"You were supposed to find out if Aaron is a murderer, or did you forget?" Avery reminded her.

"Don't worry about him," Tiffany said casually. "He's been on vacation for quite some time and got back the day after you found that guy."

"William."

"Right, William," Tiffany said. "So, there's no way that Aaron could have committed the murder. Although, that might at least have made him interesting!"

"That's no lie," Avery said. "But he also would have been dangerous."

"Enough about that. I'm tired and dying for a bath. Talk to you tomorrow."

That ended the call. Avery took a deep breath and held it for a moment. She was glad to hear Aaron had an alibi, but she still didn't trust him all that much. She took her dishes to the kitchen and headed to her laptop.

By that point, she'd already forgotten all about the food on the television.

She opened her computer and searched for Aaron's social media profiles. From what Tiffany had said, he was rather full of himself. If he had gone on vacation, she was certain he would have posted some photographs somewhere.

It didn't take her long. She found many images of him in his bathing suit. By the look of it, he had taken a long, very expensive trip. In each photograph, he struck the same pose and gave the same dazzling smile.

Each image was accompanied by another quote about success. Avery checked the dates of the posts, and they checked out. Satisfied, she closed his profile and pulled closer the page with her list of meals.

She opened up a new, blank document and checked the time. It was still early, and there were likely many hours before she would go to bed. She considered typing out a basic business plan for her restaurant.

She couldn't wait to show it to Tiffany and watch her panic about the thought of all the work that would need to go into it. But instead, she typed out her future dream menu. It would still need a lot of work, but she figured it was a good place to start.

She typed away, piecing together recipes and wine pairings. Then, she pulled out a map of the vineyard and contemplated where she could find the space to put it. The vineyard was quickly filling up.

Avery sat back and thought about it. Perhaps Tiffany was right, and she was taking on too much. She had a habit of doing that. It was a way in which she could avoid the thoughts that she didn't want to think. As long as she had something to do for her business, she didn't have to think about her own personal future. Instead of doing that, she prioritized her business and allowed it to consume all of her time.

When her phone rang again, it snapped her out of deep thought. She glanced over to see who it was and smiled when she saw Charles' name.

"I thought I'd never hear from you," she said. "Figured you'd already forgotten all about me."

"Never!" Charles said cheerfully.

"I know, I'm just teasing."

Avery walked back to the kitchen and poured herself her last glass of wine for the evening. Then she sat down on the couch next to Sprinkles.

"I'm sorry I've taken so long to get back to you," Charles said. "I've honestly been so busy at the station and so tired. Last night, I fell asleep in my clothes and shoes."

"Oh dear," Avery laughed. "That bad?"

"Yeah!" he answered. "Chief wasn't kidding when he said they needed help there."

"So, how has it been going?" Avery asked. "Is it like riding a bike? Did you walk in there and immediately know what you were doing?"

Charles laughed loudly. "Not exactly. But I'll get the hang of it again, I'm sure. Besides, I've committed to at least see this case through to the end."

"You're a man of your word, and everybody knows that," Avery said plainly. "Just be careful that people don't ask too much of you because of it."

Charles chuckled. "I'll make sure to take note of it; thanks."

"So tell me about Paul's interrogation," Avery said, nestling into her seat. "Do you think he might have done it?"

"No," Charles answered. "The interrogation was lengthy, though. He's a stubborn man. He purposefully spoke in circles to annoy me, and it worked."

"But you don't think he did it?"

"I know for a fact he didn't do it," Charles answered. "It took hours, but eventually he gave us his location for the time of the murder."

"And it checks out?"

"Yes," Charles said. "He was working late. Not only could his colleagues confirm it, but the security guard also sent us a tape from that night. He was at his desk at the time of William's murder."

"You don't seem too pleased about it," Avery said.

"Well, it took him three hours before he finally gave us a straight answer. It was a complete waste of time, and in the meantime, a murderer gets to walk freely through the streets of Los Robles."

Avery understood his frustration. It seemed like an unusually cruel thing for Paul to do.

"Why do you think he did that?" Avery asked.

"I don't know," Charles sighed. "Maybe he felt we were wasting his time too and decided to be childish about it."

"So, what now? Are there any other suspects?"

"Not at this moment, no," Charles said. "We're right back to a blank board."

"Oh, I'm sorry," Avery said.

She could hear the exhaustion in his voice. It sounded like he would fall asleep while he was still talking to her.

"Good news is, I'll be back at the wine room tomorrow."

"Charles, you don't have to do that," Avery said. "It looks like it might rain tomorrow, the wine room will be quiet."

"No, I'd like to be there," he answered. "It will be a nice change of scenery, and I can check in on Beth."

"Alright, then get some rest tonight," she instructed.

"I'm already in bed!" he said with a laugh.

They ended the call, and Avery thought about her own bed. It was earlier than she normally got into bed, but it did seem inviting. It was a cooler evening, and she could feel the cold on her skin.

Avery got into bed and realized she felt excited for the next day. It dawned on her that it might be because she knew that she would see Charles again and that they might share a laugh together.

She was excited to have his energy back at the vineyard.

Sprinkles hopped up on the bed and snuggled up close to Avery. She thought of chasing him away but changed her mind. She liked his company.

Avery closed her eyes and went to sleep easily. She didn't wake up until the sun came through her window, forcing her awake.

Chapter Ten

Avery wrapped up her work for the morning as quickly as she could and took one last glance at her emails before stepping out the door and heading toward the wine shop. It was a busy day at the vineyard as they prepared to launch their new tasting area that night.

She had a few minutes to spare, though, and an important friend to check up on. Avery walked, enjoying the blue skies that filled the space above her, despite the weather predictions of the day before.

When she entered the wine room, there he was. He looked completely exhausted. Avery slid a large cup of coffee over the counter toward him.

"Bless you," he sighed, taking the cup.

"I looked for the biggest cup I could find," she said with a smile.

Charles took a large, eager sip of the coffee and smiled.

"Let's go sit in the sun for a little while," Avery suggested.

Charles looked around the wine room to make sure that everything was in order and walked happily with Avery to a nearby bench.

"Are you sure you're up for today?" Avery said. "It will be alright if you need to take a few hours to get some sleep."

"I'll be alright," Charles said. "I can't take naps. If I get into bed now, I'll sleep until tomorrow, and there is no way I'm missing the party tonight."

"Well, at least take it easy today," Avery said. "I don't want to drag your sleeping body all the way from the pond to your car."

Charles smiled and nodded in agreement as he took another big sip.

"So, tell me about the case. You have no suspects. What kind of evidence or clues do you have?"

"Evidence?" Charles scoffed. "There is basically none. The body is clean. No skin cells, no fingerprints, nothing to help us. It's as if every inch had been wiped down."

"That's odd, right?" Avery said. "Surely that doesn't happen often?"

"No," he answered. "That never happens."

Avery looked out at the vineyard. At that moment, it was quiet and peaceful there. She glanced out over the space, her mind trying to picture where a restaurant would look best.

"The only evidence on the body is what would have gotten onto him between that cabinet and the wall," Charles said, bringing Avery's attention back to the subject at hand.

"So, that seems like a lot of work, right?" she asked.

"Oh yeah," Charles said. "Which is why it's so unusual. It would take a lot of time and a lot of effort. Most murderers are lazier than that."

"Judging by that knowledge, how long was he behind the cabinet, then?" Avery asked.

"That's what I'm trying to work out. But it is hard to say, as I cannot be certain exactly how long it would take to clean the body."

"I see," Avery said. "I suppose it isn't very helpful, is it?"

"Not very, no," Charles responded.

"And what about the cause of death?" Avery asked. "Surely that can tell you something?"

Charles took a deep breath. "It seems that William drowned."

Avery almost spat out her sip of coffee. "Drowned?" she barked. "What do you mean he drowned? He was completely dry and sandwiched between a wall and a cabinet!"

"Well, you don't have to get wet to drown," Charles explained. "Your lungs simply need to be filled with water."

Avery thought about it for a moment, but it made her head hurt.

"I'm sorry Charles, but I still don't understand how that might have happened," she said.

"The coroner could tell, from markings in his mouth, that either a funnel or a pipe had been forced into his mouth. Then, water would have been poured down it, filling his lungs."

Avery felt nauseated as she thought about it, and she suddenly no longer wanted her coffee.

"That's horrendous. How could you even get that right?"

"It would appear that he was knocked out by a blow to the head," he explained. "But the cause of death is drowning."

Avery had never heard of anything like that in her life. It seemed so cruel, so well thought through. Then, the murderer would have cleaned the body. It was as if every moment of the murder had been carefully planned.

"Well, whoever did it, they really wanted him dead, didn't they?" Avery asked.

"Yes, it appears that way," Charles said.

Avery could not believe what she was hearing. It sent a shiver down her spine. It seemed like a lot of effort to take a life. The man she had seen behind the cabinet had not been a small man. He'd been tall, and she was sure he weighed a lot. Whoever had done it had to have been exhausted afterward.

"And I suppose the murderer had to have access to the wine cave," Avery muttered.

"That's correct," Charles sighed. "It helps us know where to look, but it doesn't exactly narrow it down. From what we know, there were crews of workers there to paint and repair shelves."

"Oh," she said, disappointed.

"And it seems that almost every member of staff there had access to the farm. Never mind those who were staying in the guesthouse at the time."

"Seems like you guys have a lot of work ahead of you," Avery said. "You know, if you need more time off from the wine room, it will be alright. I know how important this decision is to you, and I don't like to see you so tired."

"No, that's alright," he answered. "I enjoy being here at the vineyard. It actually helps me unwind."

Avery smiled quietly to herself. It was the biggest compliment he could possibly have given her, and he didn't even know it. Tranquility was what she had been striving for since she had gotten there.

"I'm glad," she said softly.

"You know, it's my first proper case in a very long time. Naturally, it is a very difficult one. One of those where I worry I might never solve it."

There was a hint of defeat in his voice, and it reminded Avery of how the job might affect Charles. She knew him to have a kind and caring heart, and she had not yet considered how he would handle the tougher sides of the job, which was why he had left in the first place.

"You'll figure this out," Avery replied, trying to sound as encouraging as possible. But she wasn't sure it would work.

"I hope so," Charles said. "Whoever committed this murder clearly felt a lot of hatred. I won't sleep if they get away with it. It would only make them more dangerous."

"Do you think whoever did it would do it again?" Avery asked.

"That happens often. If the perpetrator gets away with it once, they think they can do it again. It gives them a sense of power. And whoever did this is smart," Charles explained.

Avery felt her blood cool at the thought of it. It was beyond her that anybody could take the life of another person. But she'd learned enough in her time as a writer and with her husband. She knew murderers were complicated people, so she would never dwell on it for too long.

"I better get back in there," Charles said, taking the last sip of his coffee. "There's much to do before tonight's party."

"Okay, then," Avery said. "No time for rest."

Charles chuckled as he stood up and walked toward the wine room. Avery had enjoyed their coffee break together, but Charles was bothered. She could see the emotional and physical toll that the case was taking on him and wished there was something she could do to help.

But he was right, and she was quickly running out of time that day. She hadn't been past the pond to check on things for a few hours. So, she whistled for Sprinkles to join her and headed there.

As she walked, she found it hard to believe that the day had finally arrived. It was a familiar feeling. It was how she had felt when she opened the guesthouse and when she had released her first book.

It was a mixture of excitement and trepidation. There was always the fear that nobody would show up to the event. Even though that had never happened yet. Her stomach was in a small knot as she approached the pond.

A million thoughts ran through her mind. What if they hadn't made enough progress? What if the lights didn't work? What if the band didn't show? What if there isn't enough wine?

The idea that there wouldn't be enough wine was a ridiculous one, she understood, but still it made her nervous, which in turn made her feel foolish.

~

The new tasting area was completely packed with people. There was laughter and the clinking sound of glasses being tapped together in celebration. The band played soft jazz which filtered through the air from somewhere between the trees.

The lights twinkled, the brightness of their glow ebbing and flowing softly to set the mood. Avery took a moment to stand to one side and appreciate the success of it all.

Around her, the sommeliers that Charles had trained moved graciously from table to table with trays of wine in hand. The launch was a great success, and she'd never felt so proud in her life.

In the far corner, her mother and father sat at a VIP table. There, they were treated like royalty. Every time Avery looked in their direction, they wore bright smiles. They had never seen the vineyard in such full swing.

It was like a scene from a movie. With the lights, the party, and the guests all dressed according to theme. It looked like a party for the rich and famous, and everybody seemed to have a great time. Avery could tell that by the conversations that she had overheard and the slight look of envy on the faces of the other vineyard owners who had been invited.

It was about halfway through the party when Charles came to find her.

"Having fun? Or hiding away?" he asked as he approached her.

"Taking a breather," Avery laughed. "I've answered enough questions for now."

"It's beautiful," he remarked with a smile. "It is nice to see so many guests here."

Avery nodded. "I've already got several potential party book-ings for the space. I think it is going to be bigger than we ever thought."

"Then what?" Charles laughed. "Tiffany told me about the restaurant idea."

Avery scoffed. "She's almost as bad as Deb! I'm still thinking about it. I don't know if we have the space for it anymore."

"Not unless you pull out some vines," Charles teased.

"Don't say that!" Avery responded. "That would be terrible. I would never do that."

"I know, I know. It was a bad joke."

Their conversation was cut short by a tall, handsome man with dirty blonde hair.

"This is quite the party," he said with a slight slur. "I believe you're the owner?"

The man held his hand out to Charles.

"It will be my honor to meet the man in charge," he said with a smile.

Charles raised his eyebrows. "In that case, you might want to direct your handshake to her," he said, motioning to Avery.

"Hi," Avery said with a sweet smile. Although, she wanted to laugh loudly.

"Oh," the tall man said. "Well, lovely to meet you."

"Same to you," she said, shaking his hand. "My name is Avery."

The man held her hand a little too long, stroking her knuck-les, and it made her want to immediately run away and take a shower.

"My name is Timothy," he said with a cocky smile. "You know, I worked with that guy who was murdered last week."

Chapter Eleven

Immediately, Avery knew she was dealing with a slimy character. He had that look in his eyes, and he had clearly already had too much to drink. Still, he signaled to a waitress to bring him another glass, mouthing the word, "shiraz," as she passed him.

He tapped his finger against the glass, just in case the waitress didn't know what he was referring to. It was clear in the way he had made a point to mention his connection to William, that he thought it made him special in some way.

Without Avery and Charles asking about it, he continued to talk about it.

"Yeah, he and I worked in the same building. Did either of you know him?" he asked.

Charles and Avery both shook their heads. She didn't quite think it appropriate to let him know that she had been the one to discover his body. Timothy seemed pleased with the fact that they did not know him.

"Perfect!" Timothy cheered as the waitress returned with his glass of wine.

"Enjoy," Avery said. She didn't like his character, but she needed to be a good host.

"I will, thank you," he answered, taking a rather large sip.

His lips were already stained red from the wine, and there was a slight slur in his speech.

"Yes, I knew William well," Timothy continued as if anybody had asked. "We worked together. I'm a lawyer, you see."

"Ah," Charles said as he widened his eyes. "Well done, then."

"Thank you!" Timothy said proudly. "Well, William and I weren't exactly friends. We got along when we needed to, but that wasn't often."

"Oh," Avery said with her eyebrows raised.

"I feel terribly for his family, of course. But he wasn't always the nicest person. He certainly had his enemies. You know, I bet you Paul did it. Did you hear about what William did to Paul?"

"Yes, of course," Charles said. "Everybody knows about that by now."

"Some others at the office were so sad to learn of his death," Timothy continued.

"But not you?" Charles asked with a forced smile.

"Of course, it shocked me," Timothy said. "And I was a little sad. But I quickly got used to him not being around the office. That sounds terrible, I know, I know. But hey, at least I can be honest about it."

His rambling was borderline embarrassing. Avery looked at Charles with uncertainty, but he seemed perfectly alright to keep talking. It dawned on Avery then that Timothy had just made himself a suspect.

It was an odd interaction, to say the least. Neither Charles nor Avery could figure out exactly why the conversation was happening or where it was going. He clearly didn't know that Charles was working on the case. If he did, he clearly wasn't a very good lawyer.

"Why's that?" Charles asked.

"Why's what?" Timothy drunkenly responded.

"Why didn't the two of you get along?"

"Ah," Timothy said, swaying slightly. "Workplace competition I guess you could call it. He was a talented lawyer, which meant he got all the good cases and all the good promotions."

"I see," Avery said. "So the two of you argued a lot?"

"I guess," Timothy said. "Nothing more than usual workplace drama, you guys know that I'm sure."

Avery and Charles looked at each other and shook their heads.

"No, not really," Avery answered. "I'm the boss. I don't argue with people."

Timothy burst out laughing as if he'd just heard the funniest joke ever told. It was an overreaction, that was sure. Avery cared little for the conversation, but she'd put up with it as long as Charles wanted to.

"What did you guys use to argue about?" Charles asked.

"He would get all the good clients and all the good promotions," Timothy answered. "That's what we fought about just before he...well, you know, died."

"Yeah?" Charles responded.

"Yeah! He got the promotion I was after," Timothy explained. "I mean, he got it fair and square, but I was pretty upset and said some mean things to him. I wish I could take it back sometimes. But I can't, so...that's that, I guess!"

"Fair and square?" Avery asked. "Did he often not do things fair and square?"

"Of course!" Timothy said. "He was a lawyer. He knew just how to cheat the system. That's what made him such a good lawyer, to begin with."

It seemed like every day or two, Avery was coming across another person who hadn't been a fan of the deceased. William had clearly made a lot of enemies in his life.

"Anyway, it's kind of a bummer how he died," Timothy

continued. "But I try to keep things positive. One man's loss is another man's gain as they say."

It was the last thing Avery ever expected anybody to say when talking about the death of another person. She couldn't believe how insensitive Timothy was being about it all. Yet, Timothy didn't seem to think there was anything wrong with what he was saying.

He sipped at his wine as if it was the last wine on Earth. It seemed to Avery that he was on a mission to drink as much of the free wine as he could possibly manage. He was doing well. His glass was already empty, and once again his finger was tapping against the side as he ordered yet another refill.

It had crossed her mind before to enforce a limit for her guests. The last thing she wanted was for anybody to be over-served. And Timothy was the most convincing argument for it.

"Yep," he continued. "Sometimes what sucks for one person doesn't suck so much for another. Hey, just being honest," he said again.

"What exactly do you mean by that?" Avery asked, getting frustrated with the direction that the conversation was going.

It didn't feel right to her to speak about a murder victim that way. She could put up with it so that Charles could get more information, but she hoped it wouldn't last much longer. She also didn't have to be friendly about it.

"Well, with William gone, I am next in line for that promotion," Timothy explained.

It seemed almost as if he was proud of that fact. He had a sickening smirk on his face. Avery wished she could tell him what she was thinking. But she knew Charles would want to get as much information as he possibly could. So, she bit her tongue.

Timothy's next glass of wine arrived, and he immediately started sipping at it.

"I suppose that's good news for your income," Charles said, talking in a casual manner.

Timothy nodded eagerly. "Better pay, yes, better benefits, better clients, better office, better everything!"

"Lucky you," Charles said.

"You see!" Timothy said. "Something bad happened, sure. But also, something good happened."

Timothy chuckled some more as he sipped his wine. At that point, the conversation was bothering Avery immensely.

"What kind of benefits?" Charles asked.

Timothy smiled. It was clear that he was eager for the conversation and excited to talk about it. It was as if he felt important when Charles asked him questions. The man clearly had a colossal ego, and the alcohol seemed to have ramped it up.

Avery let out a quiet sigh, just loud enough for Charles to hear. She didn't want to continue with the conversation much longer; it just didn't feel right to her.

As if her prayer had been answered, someone called his attention away from them. Timothy left without another word to greet a friend of his.

"Thank goodness," Avery said. "I was starting to get uncomfortable."

"Yes, that was rather odd," Charles said.

"He can't be a very good lawyer," Avery said. "He didn't seem concerned that he might have been incriminating himself!"

"I think that might have been caused by the alcohol," Charles said. "I think the more he sipped, the less he thought."

Avery chuckled. "That's precisely it."

Charles seemed perturbed, though.

"Do you think he's a suspect?" Avery asked.

"Well, he's showing signs of that being a possibility," Charles explained. "He spoke about it, without prompt, which is often a sign. And he had something to gain from William's death. He's got a motive."

"So, now what?" Avery asked.

"I need to tread carefully," Charles said. "He is a lawyer, and

I can get myself into a fair amount of trouble if I don't do this the right way."

"I suppose you'll have to talk to Chief Mathers first?"

"Yeah," Charles said. "But something about Timothy just doesn't sit well with me."

"Same," Avery said. "That entire encounter made me very uncomfortable. Imagine saying those things about a murder victim."

"It's more common than you think," Charles said. "Especially when there's alcohol involved. People like Timothy are, unfortunately, common."

"He would know enough to think of cleaning the body," Avery mentioned. "Being a lawyer, he'd know exactly what kind of evidence he would have to get rid of."

"That's what I was thinking too," Charles muttered. "And, you're right."

At that moment, it looked as if Timothy was headed back in their direction. Avery's heart sank. She didn't want to talk with him for another moment longer.

"Shall we go for a walk?" Charles asked. "I'm sure the party will be just fine without your presence for five minutes."

"Yes, please," Avery said. "Thank you."

With that, Charles and Avery walked away from the pond and the party and went through some of the nearby vines. They weren't the only ones with that idea. They passed a few of the partygoers trying to find a quiet place to have a conversation and enjoy the views that the vineyard had to offer.

Charles and Avery spoke about the party, talking about all the details that did work and those that didn't. They spoke of the future of the tasting area's success and what that would mean for the vineyard.

Charles listened carefully as Avery told him about her dreams of all the events that they could host there and all the ways in which the vineyard could still be changed and improved.

He smiled as she spoke, and it felt nice to have someone just listen. He didn't overwhelm her with questions or point out all the struggles she might come across.

"I think you're creating quite the empire for yourself here," Charles said. "I'm really proud of you."

"Thank you," Avery said sheepishly. "Thank you also for saving me from another conversation with Timothy, but we should probably head back. I can't be gone too long."

"Yeah," Charles said.

They spun on their heels and turned back toward the party. But Avery did slow down her pace. It felt good to step away for a moment. The quiet moment seemed to be giving her further energy for the rest of the night.

"So, is it helping you make a decision at all?" Avery asked. "You know, working on a case. Has it helped?"

Charles took a deep breath and let it out slowly.

"No, not really," he said with a laugh. "I think I need to make a little more headway with the case to know how I feel about it. At the moment, I'm just stuck, and I don't like it to be that way."

"I'm sure it's going to be just fine," she said. "Even if you do go back and decide later you don't want it anymore, just know that I'll always have a spot for you here."

"Not if Beth has anything to do with it," Charles laughed loudly. "She seems determined to run this place someday!"

He wasn't wrong. Beth had worked really hard, and each week she seemed eager to take on more responsibilities. In reality, Avery owed a lot of the success of the party to her.

"Before we get back," Charles said. "I will probably not make it through the entire party without falling asleep. So I will probably leave soon. But I just want to ask about that date I'd like to take you on."

"What about it?" Avery asked.

"Well, when would you like to go?" he asked.

As they walked the last stretch of their journey back to the party, they decided on a day and a time. Avery felt nervous about it, but the hustle and bustle of the party quickly distracted her from those feelings.

Chapter Twelve

Two days had passed since the party, and Avery still felt exhausted. The party had carried on until the early hours of the morning, and by the time they'd finished packing up and cleaning, it was almost sunrise.

Because of that, Avery closed the vineyard the next day so her staff could get some rest. Of course, so she could too. However, she had spent most of the previous day answering people responding to the event.

The reviews had been overwhelmingly positive, and she was feeling good about everything. Her father had already phoned her about six times to thank her for a wonderful evening.

Avery sat at the table at Deb's house as the women of the Stammtisch chatted merrily around her. But she had a hard time concentrating on the conversation. She'd been zoned out for some time, her glass resting comfortably in her hand.

The gray tones of Deb's house had made Avery feel calm, which only made her feel tired. But she didn't want to miss lunch. She hadn't seen the women in quite some time. They had all been at the party, but she'd been so busy with other things that she'd hardly had the chance to speak with any of them that night.

As Avery's attention came back to the room, she realized she had no idea what they were talking about anymore. So, she listened closer in hopes that she could figure it out along the way.

"I tell you what," Deb said. "I'm done with tours for some time."

They were talking about the wine cave tour Marcus had given them. Somewhere in the recesses of her mind, she could recall his name being mentioned in the conversation.

"I'm still recovering from all that," she continued. "I've had such nightmares I can't even begin to describe. At one point I considered seeing a doctor about it, but then it came to an end, thank goodness."

Eleanor nodded in agreement. "I'm not surprised. People don't normally go through that kind of thing. But it doesn't matter...all tours won't be like that."

"I know, I know," Deb said. "But I think it might be a reminder of what happened, you know? Like, it would jog my memory or whatever."

"We're not even the ones who found the body," Eleanor said.

"You're right," Deb said. "How are you doing after everything, Ave?" she asked.

It was the first time she'd given Avery a nickname, but Avery would allow it.

"I'm doing alright," Avery answered. "I've had a few nightmares too, to be honest. But they've stopped for now. I'm just pretty tired, so sorry if I've been quiet."

"That's good. I've been worried about you," Deb said. "If it had been me that had found him, I don't think I would ever have left the house again!"

"Well, I've been gratefully distracted by work, which has

helped," Avery responded. "With everything that needed to be planned, I hardly had time to think about what had happened."

"I've had some dreams too," Eleanor admitted. "Horrible dreams. Some of them I don't quite remember, but I know it was about that day."

"I haven't had any dreams," Camille piped up.

Her voice broke the silence, finally making its presence known after an entire day of silence. Surprisingly, it appeared that Camille had brushed off the events without a care in the world. It was almost as if she had effortlessly let go of it the moment she walked away from the vineyard.

"That's good," Deb said. "You're lucky!"

"It was a terrible thing," Tiffany said. "But the rest of that day was pretty good, and we all drank some really good wine."

The women all agreed eagerly. For the next few minutes, they each shared the dreams that they'd had as if they had been comparing notes. With each story, the dreams seemed to be getting worse and worse and more descriptive.

The only one of them with nothing to say was Camille, as always.

Each dream that was told was broken down into small chunks as the women tried to decipher what the meaning of each detail might have been. Eventually, Deb ran to her bookshelf and pulled out a book she had on dreams.

They took turns looking up the individual details of their dreams and came to the conclusion that they had all been somewhat traumatized by the event. Although, Avery knew they didn't need a book to figure that one out.

Eventually, lunch was served. Avery has always had a soft spot for pizza, and today's barbeque chicken pizza was extra satisfying. It was exactly what Avery was in the mood for. She ate it eagerly as the subject of the murder continued.

"I bet you it was Paul," Deb said. "You guys know what William did to Paul, don't you?"

Eleanor sighed. "Everyone knows what he did to Paul, it was all over the news and people spoke about it for weeks. Just like with that whole restaurant situation of his."

"Yeah," Tiffany said. "But like I told you guys earlier, I went on a date with that guy, and there's no way he did it."

"That only leaves Paul then," Deb said seriously.

"He was a lawyer," Avery laughed. "I'm sure he had many enemies, and many people who were unfriendly toward him. He probably put people in jail!"

"Yes!" Deb said, getting excited. "It is probably someone he put away that got to him in the end. That's it!"

"Whoever it is, they'd have needed access to that bookshelf," Eleanor said.

It quickly dulled Deb's spirit as she realized that a released convict likely didn't work at a vineyard like that one.

It seemed to Avery that Paul and Aaron had been William's claim to fame. It certainly was all that the community knew him for. He had to have helped at least some people, but nobody seemed to talk about those people.

Instead, they focused on the negative.

"I spoke with Marcus earlier today, by the way," Deb said between bites.

"How is he doing?" Eleanor asked. "I'm sure he must have a hard time. He had to sleep on that property! I could never. I'd be too afraid that it might be haunted."

"Actually, he's still quite rattled by the entire ordeal," Deb shared. "He confesses that entering that place has become a real challenge for him. He tries to stay up late, pushing himself to complete his tasks, just to avoid facing the constant inquiries from others about what happened."

Avery could sympathize with him.

"That is upsetting," Tiffany said. "I wonder how long he will feel that way or if he'll ever feel comfortable there again."

"Do you think he'll sell the place?" Eleanor asked.

Deb shrugged. "That vineyard has been in his family for generations. It would take a lot to get him to leave."

"Still, he might, don't you think?" Tiffany asked. "I could never live anywhere a dead body was found."

"Me neither," Deb said. "But he feels an attachment to that place. Who knows? Maybe with some therapy or something he can feel comfortable there again."

"Maybe we should all go to therapy," Camille piped up, on a rare occasion when she spoke twice. "You know, we all saw it too."

"We can go together!" Deb said excitedly. "A group session!"

"I know a friend who could do it!" Eleanor chimed in.

Anybody watching might have thought that they were planning a weekend away. There was so much excitement at the thought of all of them going to therapy together, it was completely ridiculous.

Nobody took it seriously, of course, but still, they continued on with the conversation. Likely hoping it might steer the conversation in a more positive direction. But Avery couldn't stop thinking about Marcus. She hadn't even considered what he must have been going through. In fact, after that day, she had almost forgotten about him.

He had been the only invited person not to attend her party. She figured perhaps he was exhausted and didn't want to have to talk about the incident with so many people. She was okay with that. But she felt poorly for him and what he was going through.

The rest of the conversation at Deb's house was a lot more positive. They spoke of relationships and holidays. Eleanor spoke of the recent renovations to her home, and Deb dropped the shocking news that she might paint one of the walls in her house a color other than gray.

The women finished their lunch and wine and then hopped into their respective cabs to head home. It was late afternoon by the time Avery was on her way back to her home and, as she sat quietly in the back of the cab, she passed the vineyard where Marcus lived.

Her thoughts moved over to him, and she wondered if he was okay and what he was doing that afternoon. Avery considered going over to see him and check on him and show him some positive support.

She understood how important it could be. It could help her integrate into the community more, which had been one of her goals for that season. She knew that if she wanted her business to thrive, she'd have to make a name for herself among the locals. She only hoped it would be a better name than the one that William had made for himself.

When Avery got home, she made a note in her calendar that she would pay Marcus a visit the next day and perhaps take another special bottle of Le Blanc Cellars reserve wine for his collection as a token of kindness.

It was the only thing she could think of that she knew he would definitely like.

Her phone rang. "Hi, Dad," she answered cheerfully.

"I'm just phoning to thank you again for the party and the special treatment we received," he said.

"You're welcome, Dad," Avery laughed. "But you really have thanked me enough."

"Not according to me!" he said. "You don't understand. Your mother and I have not been to such a big party in many years. It almost made us feel younger!"

"That's good news!" Avery teased.

"It is!" her father agreed. "Your mother has even invited some people over here this weekend. Now, she wants to party every week!"

"Oh dear, I've unleashed a monster," Avery said.

"Yes, well, she wanted me to phone and ask you if you wanted to join us. She's making her famous lentil soup," he explained.

"Is that the one that's that awful brown color?" Avery asked, thinking back to a memory from her childhood.

"That's the one!" he answered.

"Oh, in that case, no thanks!" Avery laughed. "But thank you for the invitation."

"I figured that would be the answer," he chuckled. "You've never liked that soup."

"Well, that, and I have a lot to do this weekend," she said.

"It's okay, I won't tell your mother that it is because of the soup," her father whispered.

"Thanks," she mumbled, knowing full well that her mother was likely standing right next to him the entire time.

"Well, talk to you later, then!" her father said right before hanging up.

Avery noticed an unread message on her phone from Charles.

I slept most of the day away yesterday. I feel much better and well-rested. Thanks for the day off, boss!

She smiled as she made her way to the kitchen to pour herself a cup of coffee. She'd had half a glass too many at Deb's house, and she had still wanted to do some brainstorming about her future restaurant.

The coffee was meant to sort her out, and she hoped it would work. She wanted to look at the map again and find any amount of space she had left for a structure. By the time she made it to her laptop, Sprinkles was already curled up on the rug where her feet would be, waiting for her.

Chapter Thirteen

Avery arrived at Marcus' vineyard and couldn't shake the heavy feeling that hung over her. It was likely because of the experience she'd had the last time that she'd been there. Thankfully, she had Sprinkles at her side to keep her company as she approached the reception area.

Sprinkles was excited about being there, and he stopped to sniff everything along the way to greet everybody they passed. One of those people was a woman who looked familiar to Avery, despite her knowing that they had never met before.

The woman passed her and flashed Avery a warm smile, and as Avery walked, she wondered where she could have seen the woman before.

It was bothering her, and she could not get herself to let it go.

She was right outside the reception when it dawned on her. She'd seen the woman before in all the photographs she'd seen online when she was looking up William.

It was his wife, the ex-wife of Paul. She was the woman who had been at the center of one of the biggest scandals that Los

Robles had ever seen. There was no doubt in her mind that it was Katrina, William's wife.

Avery stopped and turned back to see if she could catch a glimpse of her again, but she was too late. The woman was too far away to see. It gave Avery an uneasy feeling. She couldn't imagine why she would have been there at the place where her husband's dead body had been found.

Avery, having lost her own husband, had some understanding of what the woman would have been going through. Why would she have been back there? And why on Earth would she have been smiling about it, too?

It was completely perplexing to Avery, who didn't want to think about it too much. She wanted to see Marcus, give him the wine, tell him she was thinking of him, and get out of there.

The more she walked on the property, the more uneasy she felt about it all. She kept remembering what William's face looked like when she found him behind that cabinet.

Avery shook her head in an attempt to end her thoughts. There had to have been a good reason for William's wife to have been there, and perhaps she handled grief better than Avery had.

Just because it made little sense to her didn't mean that it was something to suspect.

Sprinkles had run ahead of Avery and was pestering some people at a nearby table, so it distracted Avery from her confusion as she went to call him back. Then, she was at the reception and merely focused on the task at hand.

When she stepped inside, she found Marcus was already there.

Had he been talking with William's wife? If so, what would they have been talking about?

Avery reminded herself it was none of her business and that she had gone there that day for a reason.

"Marcus," she said with a smile. "Just the man I am looking for."

"Avery!" he greeted her warmly. "What a pleasant surprise! What can I do for you?"

"I've actually just come to give you something and to check on you and see how you're doing," Avery said, handing him the bottle of wine.

Marcus inspected the label, and a wide smile broke across his face.

"This is really special, thank you," he said kindly. "Why don't you walk with me, and we'll add it to my collection together?"

"Sure," Avery said.

She called for Sprinkles to follow, and the three of them walked out the door and toward his collection room. His vineyard was in full swing, and he greeted people cheerfully as he passed them.

Avery admired his ability to keep his smile and his professional demeanor given the fact that he apparently wasn't coping at all with what had happened.

"How have things been going here?" she asked.

"Oh, just swell," he said. "It's the busiest season we've had in many years. Although, I do think the bad press had something to do with it."

He said it with hardly a shred of emotion behind his words. He had nothing to hide from Avery, as she had been there. The two of them were alone at that point.

"So sorry to have missed your party, by the way," he continued. "I believe it was quite the roaring success. I'm hearing only excellent reviews of that tasting room."

"No need to apologize," she said. "I figured it might not have been an inviting idea to be faced with so much of the community after everything that happened."

"Why do you say that?" he asked with a puzzled look.

"Well, they'd be asking questions and things like that," she explained. "I thought perhaps you'd want to avoid all that."

"Oh no," he said calmly. "A family member I haven't seen in quite some time was in town, so I made plans to see him. I wanted to let you know, but it completely slipped my mind."

"That's alright," Avery said uneasily.

Something about his attitude bothered her. There seemed to be no concern from him at all, and he seemed completely unbothered by what had happened. Which was the opposite of what Deb had been telling them the day before.

"How are you doing?" Avery asked.

"Oh, I'm good," he said happily. "Busy as always, but having a good time with it. It's one of the many perks of loving my job. I'm sure you understand that."

"I do," she said with a nervous chuckle. "I spend way too much of my time working, some say."

"Nonsense," Marcus laughed, waving his hand through the air as if to wave away her words. "You work hard for your success, and it shows."

Avery wanted to ask him what William's wife was doing there. She just couldn't shake a feeling in her gut that something odd was going on.

As they walked through the vineyard, Avery had completely lost sight of Sprinkles. He'd run off into the vines and was happily chasing some crickets and bugs. Avery didn't like him going too far from her. She knew that if he found a body of water, he'd likely jump headfirst into it. It was not in her schedule to give him a bath that day.

So, she whistled for her trusty dog to get back to her side. But Sprinkles didn't come. Avery could hear her dog nearby as he played, but no matter how much she called him, he did not come.

Eventually, she broke from the conversation to go get him, attaching his lead so that he wouldn't wander off again. But as she returned to Marcus, she noticed a change in Sprinkles' behavior.

He cowered and growled softly, placing himself between her and Marcus.

"Sprinkles!" Avery reprimanded him. "You're being rude! This is a friend."

But Sprinkles did not stop. He remained that way. Avery tried everything they had done in their training. Sprinkles kept his eyes on Marcus and wouldn't let him out of his sight.

"I'm sorry about this," Avery said, confused. "All this time I thought I had him pretty well trained. But I suppose not. He usually listens to me."

Marcus smiled kindly at her.

"Don't worry," he said. "It's not you, it's me. This happens all the time."

It was an odd statement, to say the least. But Sprinkles would not relent. She kept his lead wrapped around her hands. Her dog would not even let her walk. He lay down on her feet and wouldn't budge.

"Most dogs react to me this way," Marcus said. "Ever since I was a child. I guess I'm just not a dog person."

Avery decided to simply ignore it and finish up her conversation as quickly as she could. She wiggled her feet free, and they continued with their walk, Sprinkles walking between them.

"How were things after we all left the other night?" Avery asked, getting to the reason she was there. "I've actually come to make sure that you're alright."

It looked as if a switch had been flipped in Marcus. He cleared his throat and dropped his smile. His eyes moved down to look at the ground in front of him.

"Well, the police were here for days afterward," he drawled. "I wondered if people would ever come back here again. But instead, it's made us busier than ever."

"I spoke to Deb, and she said you were quite shaken," Avery said.

"Oh, yeah," he answered. "It's not a pleasant thing to deal

with, of course. All my staff were being called in for questioning, and some of them have left, refusing to work here anymore."

"I'm sorry," she said.

"What's worse is that I already have an inbox full of requests from paranormal investigators to come and look for spirits. I didn't even know that was a thing. One of them even said I could get money from doing tours. It's sick," he said.

"That is awful," Avery said. "I mean, they could at least wait some time before they ask."

Marcus nodded.

She observed Marcus as they spoke. His cheerful mood had completely changed, nevertheless, as he spoke, he chuckled from time to time. Avery found his behavior to be strange, and she couldn't quite figure out why.

But she pushed that thought from her mind. She understood everyone dealt with stress in different ways and that perhaps she was overthinking it.

"How are you doing after everything?" he asked. "I mean, I think you had it the worst out of all of us."

Avery shrugged. "I've had some nightmares about it. But I think that's normal when things like this happen."

"I suppose," Marcus said with a smile.

"I keep trying to figure out who did it," she confessed. "Even though it isn't my place. The work I did with my husband, the books I've recently written...I can't seem to help myself."

"I can believe that," Marcus said. "I read your last book. It was pretty good!"

"Thanks," Avery said meagerly.

"Have you heard anything about the case?" he asked. "I keep phoning the police, but nobody will give me any answers. They say they can't tell me. But it happened on my property. Surely I deserve to know?"

The temptation to tell him what she knew was strong. But

Avery understood that if the police didn't want to tell him anything, then there was likely a good reason for it.

"No," she lied. "I haven't heard anything. But I have faith in our police and that they'll solve this case."

Marcus looked toward the wine cave.

"It's just hard to believe that something so terrible could happen somewhere so beautiful," Marcus said.

Finally, they were in the collection room, and her bottle was placed among the rest of them. Avery took that as her opportunity to leave. Sprinkles was still misbehaving, and she felt guilty.

Avery felt that she had broken Marcus' good mood from earlier that day by reminding him that something terrible had happened on his property. It hadn't been her intention. She merely had hoped to extend a caring hand.

"Thank you again for the gift," he said as they approached the parking lot.

"You're so welcome," Avery said. "It's a good place for it."

As soon as Marcus left, Sprinkles went back to his usual good behavior. Avery had to agree with Marcus at that moment. He clearly was not a dog person. She secured Sprinkles onto the back seat of her car and headed home.

She wondered if it had been worth her while at all to go there and check on Marcus. She hoped he would at least find his way back to the cheerful mood he had been in when she had first gotten there.

Chapter Fourteen

When Avery got home from her visit to Marcus, she had a hard time shaking the uneasy feeling she had about it. She was glad she could show support and check in on him, but her feelings of guilt only grew stronger the more she thought about how quickly his demeanor had changed when she brought up the topic of the event.

To clear her mind, she went to her laptop with the idea of doing some work. But much to her surprise, one of her team members had already done it for her. It was exactly what she had wanted for that year. But now that she'd reached that point, she found herself more bored than she'd ever been.

Avery poured herself a cup of coffee and got through the little work that she needed to do for that day. It seemed ridiculous to her to run such a large vineyard and still find herself with nothing to do.

But it was a weekday just after the event, so a quiet day would have been normal. Still, she had too much energy for a quiet day that day. Her work took her all of one hour to get through, and then she was back to square one. As much as it was a bad idea, she poured herself another cup of coffee.

Avery walked along the bookshelf, hoping that a book would jump out at her and she could spend the afternoon reading, but that didn't happen. Nothing seemed to inspire her.

She looked out the window in the direction of the new tasting area and decided she would go take a look to see how it was doing. With a quick whistle, she had Sprinkles at her side, and they walked merrily together toward the pond.

It was a lovely warm day with a cool breeze. She could hear the breeze rushing through the treetops on the edge of the property. Birds sang and flew overhead, and the vines smelled like home to her. She took a deep breath in and reminded herself that there was enjoyment in the business around her, even if she wasn't a part of it.

She paused a moment before finishing her walk to the pond and new tasting area. She hadn't yet thought about how she might feel if she found it empty. It was the first week of it being open, and she had hoped for it to be a success.

But she had been alive long enough to know that success wasn't always a given. She prepared herself for the worst. Avery pictured what the space looked like without a single person seated, the waitresses leaning casually against the bar with nothing to do.

The thought of it freaked her out, but she prepared for the worst and then carried on walking. The nearer she got to the space, the more she could hear the sound of laughter and chatter.

When she arrived, she was pleased to find all but three tables occupied and filled with wine glasses. Her heart threatened to leap right out of her throat as she saw the place in full swing.

It was barely after lunchtime and should have been quieter than it was. At the furthest table from her, she spotted the wine critic who wrote for the local paper. Beth was paying close attention to her table, and she seemed to be all smiles.

All of Avery's concerns melted away at that moment. It was a success. Avery didn't want to disrupt the process there, so she snapped an image of the moment on her phone and turned back toward her home.

Sprinkles walked easily at her side and on his best behavior. He was completely different from how he had been just a few hours before when they'd been walking with Marcus. It puzzled Avery. As she walked, she realized perhaps Sprinkles had been acting out because he wanted some more attention from her.

So, when they got back to her house, she ran him through his training exercises. She loved the way Sprinkles smiled when she went through his exercises with him. By the time they were done, his tongue was hanging out the side of his mouth from being tired.

Avery gave him some water and a treat, and he curled up in his bed and went right to sleep.

She poured herself another cup of coffee and looked at her laptop. Despite not having decided whether she would write another book, she had an immense curiosity about the case and the characters involved.

She pulled her chair closer to her table and searched for Timothy on social media. He wasn't hard to find, as he had almost everybody in Los Robles listed as his friend. There, she saw a post he made pretending to be sad about the passing of William.

In the very next post, he wrote about his new promotion.

She clicked on William's name, and, to her surprise, his profile was still active. It didn't feel right, snooping into the life of the deceased. But she found she could not stop herself from scrolling through the posts.

There were many in which people wrote about his death and how much he would be missed. When she had finally made it through those posts, she found some that he had posted in the weeks leading up to his death.

It was strange to follow the life of a dead stranger so closely.

But there was something incredibly intriguing about it, too. Most of what William posted were images of what he was wearing to court that day and photographs of him and Katrina together.

They seemed to have lived an extravagant life, going on many exotic vacations and buying large, expensive gifts for each other. The couple seemed perfectly happy. In some of the images, they wore such big smiles that Avery couldn't help but smile too.

Then, she found an image of them together in Bali and noticed that there were over thirty comments on the photograph. She scrolled a little further and noted that other posts of his weren't getting quite as much attention.

So, she scrolled back up intending to read through the comments. There, she saw someone named Oliver Gadling. Clearly, he was a relative of the deceased.

As Avery scrolled through the comments, it was clear that the two had been arguing. It seemed they had been arguing over money. Oliver felt that the money William was spending wasn't his to spend.

When Avery opened Oliver's profile, she found a long string of posts in which he was badmouthing William. It didn't take long for her to learn that their argument had been over an inheritance battle.

William's grandfather had passed and left all his money and one of his homes to William. This had clearly angered his brother. Avery couldn't stop reading, even though it was upsetting to her to read it.

The way Oliver was talking about his brother was just terrible. He called him names and accused him of having changed his grandfather's will to exclude the rest of the family. From what Avery could tell, the brothers hadn't been on speaking terms for many years.

The language Oliver used was horrendous. He clearly had

the intention of upsetting William and turning people against him.

At that moment, the doorbell rang. It was a brilliant distraction and just what she needed to pull her away from the screen. Avery opened the door and found her dad smiling at her with half a cake in his hand.

"Hello, darling," he greeted, pushing past her and straight toward the kitchen.

"Hi, Dad! Mom baked a cake, I guess?"

"Yep!" he called from the kitchen. "As usual, half is yours."

By the time Avery joined him in the kitchen, he already had the water boiling for some tea. He sat heavily in one of the kitchen chairs, and Avery joined him.

"Would you like a slice?" she offered.

"Oh, yes," he answered. "Just don't tell your mother. I've already had two slices at home. It is very good!"

Avery laughed and cut them some cake, serving it with two warm cups of tea. She was happy to see her father.

"I've been past the pond," her father said. "It's packed!"

"I know," Avery laughed. "Isn't it wonderful?"

"I've been meaning to ask you," he said with a frown. "The other night, at the party, I saw you and Charles go for a little walk alone. What's up with that?"

Avery sipped on her tea to wash down the first bit of cake.

"Your mom says it's none of my business, but I thought I'd ask anyway," her father said before she could answer.

"I was trying to avoid a sleazy guy that was making strange conversation," Avery answered. "You're right. This is a good cake."

"That's an awfully long walk to avoid someone," her father said with a knowing smile.

Her father always knew when she was hiding something, and it occurred to her at that moment that she was too old to be embarrassed in front of her parents.

"You know, he asked me out on a date," Avery said.

"And?"

"I agreed. But we've yet to go on it."

Her father thought it over as he chewed on another bite of cake.

"Are you sure it's appropriate?" he asked. "I mean, you are his boss after all."

"That is something I've been thinking about lately," she answered. "I want to go on a date with him, but I need to do the right thing for my business, too. I've put everything into this vineyard."

"That would be my concern too," her father said.

"He's considering joining the police force again, did you know? But he hasn't decided yet."

"I didn't know that," her father said. "That certainly would solve the problem, wouldn't it?"

"It would solve one problem and cause another," she answered. "I'd lose him as a valuable employee here."

"I suppose," her father said. "But everybody can be replaced. Workplace romance is always a tricky thing. You'll feel too weird about reprimanding him."

Avery flashed him a sassy look. "Might I remind you that Mom was your assistant when you met her?"

Her father shrugged. "That was different."

"Was it?" she teased.

"Yes, and I solved that problem," her father said, eating the last bite of his cake.

"How did you solve it?"

Her father chuckled. "I fired your mother and married her instead," he answered.

Avery laughed. She could never imagine firing Charles. The thought had never even crossed her mind.

"It worked in my favor," her father shrugged.

"I suppose," Avery said. "But I am miles away from ever even thinking about marrying again."

"Well, I'm sorry to tell you but humans have little control over those feelings," her father said. "Anyway, I'd best be off. I promised your mom I'd clean out the bird bath today. It's the only thing on the calendar, so she'll be wanting it done soon."

"Thanks for bringing the cake," Avery said with a chuckle.

She hugged her father at the door and watched him take a few steps before turning back to her.

"Sometimes the answers come when we stop searching so hard for them," he said. "When we search too hard, we miss them as they pass us by."

With those kind but unhelpful words, he left to go back home.

Avery went back inside and cut herself a second slice of cake. She enjoyed it, sharing a small bite with Sprinkles with the agreement that he wouldn't tell anyone about it. She thought about what her father had said and agonized over it until her head hurt.

Chapter Fifteen

Avery had been deep in thought for almost an hour after her father left before she finally snapped out of it. He had reminded her of a reality that she could no longer ignore. As much as she didn't like what he had to say, he was right.

Avery took their dishes to the sink and then made her way back to her laptop. There, she continued to scroll through Oliver's profile. It seemed that for the past few years, his posts had been solely about William and their falling out. It had become an obsession for him.

There had to be more to it. It couldn't have just been an inheritance battle, could it? Avery had seen families go through it before, but she had never seen it to such an extent. Oliver hadn't gone a single day without bad-mouthing his brother online. That took effort.

The further she scrolled down the posts, the more she learned about just how intense the struggle between the brothers had been. That's when she learned Oliver had taken William to court over the money.

So, Avery opened a new tab and searched for any information pertaining to that court appearance. She found one small article. The article explained William had represented himself.

Oliver had accused William of doctoring the inheritance paperwork as he had been made the executor of the will. The trial wasn't long. Oliver simply had no evidence to support it. All he had was a hunch.

It took little for William to win the case. In fact, it was listed as one of the shortest cases to ever have come through that court-house. Avery chuckled at the thought of something so ridiculous happening between the brothers.

She imagined them shouting at each other across the courtroom.

"What a mess," she whispered to herself.

She went back to Oliver's social media profile and scrolled further up to see what he had said after the trial. As she expected, he started accusing William of further crimes. Oliver claimed that William and the judge were friends and that the judge had clearly been offered a cut of the inheritance money.

Oliver's profile page read like something one would see on a conspiracy platform. He had what he claimed were leads and proof that he had clearly come up with on his own. He would post photographs of the judge, accusing him publicly of taking bribes.

The sun was starting to set, and Avery was only becoming more invested in the drama that was unfolding in front of her. So, she hurried over to her kitchen and poured herself a glass of cabernet sauvignon to keep her company as she continued her deep dive into the lives of the brothers.

She made herself a snack of crackers and cheese as well and put on some soft music. Sprinkles still slept deeply as she sat back down in front of her laptop. She read through Oliver's rambling posts about how the justice system had failed him and how everything could be bought with the right amount of money.

Then, he did something that even Avery couldn't believe. He took his theories and his stories to the paper and paid for a full-page article in which he bad-mouthed his brother. Avery's jaw dropped open as she read the article.

He accused his brother of multiple crimes and mentioned Katrina in the mix as well. There he placed images of the judge and William enjoying a coffee together at the coffee shop outside the law firm where William worked.

The audacity of the news article was astounding. Avery went back to Oliver's profile and read even more. To no surprise at all, William pressed charges over it. He took Oliver to court for defamation of character. To no further surprise, won the case.

Avery chuckled as if she was pleased with the outcome. As much as she didn't like what William had done to Paul, she liked what Oliver was doing even less. What surprised her most was that the defamation suit hadn't changed anything.

Oliver continued his online abuse toward his brother for months afterward. In fact, the language he used with William only got worse. But at least, the accusations stopped.

Avery couldn't imagine talking about family in that way or taking any of her family members to court over something like an inheritance. One thing was evident. The brothers didn't care about each other one bit.

There were some friends of Oliver's who commented on his rambling posts, showing support. But most of the responses he got were from people urging him to stop and forget about it.

She looked at his profile information and saw that he only had around twelve friends listed, which didn't surprise her. His audience was small. Who did he think was listening?

It didn't make sense, but then again, he seemed to be nothing more than a very angry man who didn't know when to stop. She knew how dangerous men like that could be. It had been the premise of almost every one of the antagonists in her husband's books.

Anger and obsession made a bad pairing. From what she could tell, he was a very angry, very obsessed man. It caused more than a bit of concern in her. She scribbled his name down in her notebook, reminding her to talk to someone about it the next day.

He certainly had a motive for killing William, and she didn't want to keep quiet about it.

Avery couldn't take any more of it. She drank the last drops of her wine and closed her laptop.

A few minutes later, she was lying comfortably in bed thinking over everything she had learned that day about William and his relationship with his brother. Then she thought about her father's visit.

She got stuck on his words about Charles. Her father was right, and she knew it. Even if it wasn't what she wanted to hear. Sprinkles hopped up onto the bed and lay across her feet.

Avery trusted her father more than anyone, and it had always been that way. He had made a point of asking her about the walk, which meant that it was obvious to him what was happening when he saw them walking together.

Did that mean it was obvious to everyone else too? It was the last thing Avery wanted. She needed her staff to take her seriously and to trust her when she said things to them.

She couldn't risk them thinking that Charles might be getting away with things because they were seeing each other or that he might get special treatment from her. It was bad for business. What was bad for business, was bad for her.

She lay there for some time as she tried to decide what should be done about it. Avery didn't have the answers yet, but she had some time to think. Her head hurt from it all, and she didn't want to have to make the decision.

She dreamed that someone else could make that decision for her, even though she knew it was impossible. When she finally got the clarity she wanted, she understood that she'd had the answer the entire time. In reality, she knew exactly what to do.

It wasn't long after that when Avery and Sprinkles both fell into a deep sleep. That night, Avery's dreams were filled with bizarre courthouse scenes and conspiracy theories.

It was early morning as Avery waited in the coffee shop for Charles to join her. He didn't have much time, but she'd invited him to join her before he started his day at the precinct.

She was nervous, though. Two cups of coffee sat before her, the steam swirling through the air. It smelled delicious, but she could barely get herself to take a sip. Avery was there to break Charles' heart, even though she really didn't want to.

It had taken courage for her to set up the meeting and then even more courage to go there to meet him. In the end, she'd been so nervous that she'd arrived almost thirty minutes early.

So, for thirty minutes, she'd been agonizing over what she was going to say to him. But there were only a few minutes left before he was meant to join her. So, she needed to come up with something fast.

But those minutes were not gifted to her. Charles arrived early.

"A cup already waiting," he said with a smile. "Thank you so much."

"Of course," she said. "You mentioned you have little time. I wanted to make sure you at least were able to finish your coffee before you have to go."

"Yeah, Chief wants me in early to go over the facts again," he said. "It will be the third time that we'll be getting together to go over the facts."

Avery chuckled. "How are things going with all of that? Feeling any more confident in the case?"

"In the case? No," he answered. "But the more I work on it, the more I am comfortable doing police work again."

"I suppose you haven't yet decided about whether you'll make the permanent switch back to the force?"

"Not yet. But I keep thinking about it. Still, the answer doesn't come. I'd like for the answer to drop out of the sky, but I realize it's wishful thinking."

Their lighthearted conversation was putting Avery a bit more at ease, and she could stomach a sip of coffee. Charles talked about his days at the precinct and the days at the vineyard as they caught up on what they had missed out on.

Avery told him about her strange morning with Marcus.

"It's kind of you to have gone to check on him," Charles said.

"I hope he saw it that way," she answered. "I hope he didn't think I was there to pry."

"I doubt that's what he was thinking," Charles said with a smile.

There was some silence between them. Avery knew there wasn't much time left, she'd have to come out with it, eventually. The thought of that killed her appetite again. So, she placed her coffee back down in front of her.

"What's wrong?" Charles asked. "You never put your coffee down until it is finished. Is something bothering you? Is the coffee bad? Mine's pretty good."

Avery sighed. It was time to come out with it. "I've been thinking about our date," she said.

"Yes?"

"I just don't think it's entirely appropriate, you know?" she said. "And it's not that I don't want to go on a date with you. I really do. But I need to think of my business, and I am your boss. It just...won't look good."

Charles was silent as he took another sip of his coffee.

"It sounds bad, but you know I don't mean anything by it,"

she said. "I have to think of the vineyard and what my staff think of me. Otherwise, I couldn't possibly be a good leader for them. I hope you understand?"

Charles smiled weakly. "Avery, I understand," he said. "And you're right. It would be inappropriate. But I'd be lying if I said I wasn't a little bummed out about it."

"I'm sorry," she mumbled. "I feel terrible."

"Don't," Charles said kindly. "You're doing what's right for you. I could never be upset with you for that."

There was no more time left for them to talk about it. Charles checked his watch and realized he was already late. So, they said their goodbyes, and Charles ran out the door. Avery sat and watched her coffee get cold as she agonized over every word that was said.

Eventually, she went home to sulk a little.

Chapter Sixteen

When Avery got home, she felt like she was on autopilot. Her body functioned without any help from her brain as she poured coffee and went about her usual morning chores.

By the time mid-morning came around, she no longer knew how many cups of coffee she'd already drunk, and most of her work had already been completed. There was only one thing occupying her mind.

She was disappointed that she needed to cancel her date with Charles. It didn't feel good to do, and she felt as if she had hurt her friend. As much as he had been understanding about it, she felt guilty for how it had happened.

It felt as if they hadn't had the chance to complete their conversation before he needed to leave, so she didn't feel clear about where she stood with him. There were too many words left unsaid, so instead of focusing on the tasks at hand, she replayed imaginary versions of the same conversation repeatedly in her mind. Not that it mattered. She could not go back and change anything.

Her day felt dull.

By the time her mind rejoined her body in the real world, her hands were shaking from a caffeine overload, and her mind could barely keep her thoughts straight anymore. She hadn't eaten yet, either, which likely had something to do with it all.

But as she thought about food, she found she wasn't even all that hungry.

Avery checked her phone for a message from Charles, as she had done about fifty times that morning already. There was no message, which wasn't surprising. She didn't know what she wanted him to say, either.

He was allowed to be disappointed by it all. He was allowed to take some time to think. She just wished he wouldn't because she wanted it to be over. But not hearing from him made it impossible for her to quiet her mind of it all.

Avery wondered if she should message him first. However, when she opened the chat box, she realized she didn't know what to say. There was only one tried and tested and proven way that Avery knew she could snap out of it.

Despite it being the middle of the day, she hopped in the shower and allowed the warm water to wash her mind of its anguish and clear enough space for concentration. There was still much to do, and she was tired of her feelings that day.

It worked. When she hopped out of the shower, she found her thoughts to be crystal clear and without any direction at all.

She sat down in front of her computer and checked her social media for any updates on her friends in the city. But when she clicked the tab, it was still open on Oliver's profile. Just like that, she was sucked back into the drama that was his relationship with William.

She scrolled for half an hour as she read through the ramblings and found it a good way to distract herself from her own issues because at least it wasn't as bad as what she was reading on her screen.

Sprinkles came in and lay at her feet as he always did when she was at her laptop.

Avery scrolled and scrolled until she had no idea how far back she had gone. Then something caught her eye on the side of the screen. It was the name of one of Oliver's friends. In fact, he was listed as a family member.

Jack Gadling.

Avery clicked on the name and opened the profile. This was a man with an uncanny resemblance to William. His image showed him smiling widely on a boat somewhere on bright blue oceans.

He sported an expensive watch and a large bottle of champagne. He had thousands of people listed as his friends on his profile, and it seemed he liked to live a high life. As Avery scrolled, she learned that Jack was William's son.

It explained the resemblance.

There wasn't much posted about his father's death. There was a brief announcement that it had happened and that Jack didn't want to talk about it. However, despite it not having been long since his father had passed, Jack seemed to have moved on rather quickly.

Within hours of posting about his father's death, he had posted a joke about the government, followed by images of him and his girlfriend shopping together. Avery, unsettled by it, scrolled back to the post about his father's death and opened the comments section.

Most of it was what she expected to see, and then she stopped at one. It was a comment from Oliver.

Do you think either of us will be invited to the funeral?

Could it be possible that there were two family members so close to William who were on such bad terms with him? Avery had to know what was going on.

She narrowed her search on his profile to show any posts that mentioned his father, and she found many. Most of them were nasty.

It wasn't hard to spot that he was a bit of a spoiled brat. As were most of his friends, it seemed. From what Avery could tell, they agreed with whatever Jack had to say, no matter how cruel or outlandish it was.

Avery wasn't sure she wanted to read more, but she couldn't help herself. She needed to know what happened between William and Jack. It took a few minutes, but she eventually figured it out.

It happened about a year ago. She found what seemed to be screen captures of a conversation between William and Jack. It had been posted online for the entire world to see.

The conversation depicted a scene in which Jack had wrecked his Bentley, and William had punished him by cutting him off financially. Avery looked up any reports of a road accident from that time and found one article that featured Jack's name.

It appeared to her that Jack would regularly get into serious accidents and would often spend a night or two in jail as a result. Of course, William's name was printed in the article. It made it seem as if William had been an inadequate father and used his pull as a lawyer to get his son off the hook.

It certainly explained William's anger in the screen captures Jack had posted. She went back to Jack's profile and read through only a few of his posts. He blamed his father for everything that had gone wrong in his life.

Some posts even went as far as to say that because William had cut him off from his money, Jack would likely have to live on the streets and starve to death. It certainly was far more dramatic than it needed to be.

Avery remembered once when she was young and she bumped her father's car, scratching the side door. He'd been pretty upset, and he had punished her for it. She had to work to pay him back for the damages.

But there had never been any hatred between them for it. Then again, if she had wrecked multiple cars that he had paid for, she was certain their relationship would also have been rocky.

It was clear Jack felt his father had abandoned him and left him without any support or help.

Avery couldn't read anymore. It made her uncomfortable, and it was upsetting to see a family so torn apart by something as fickle as money. But what she knew was that both Jack and Oliver were very good suspects in the murder.

They both had motives and anger. She considered the fact that Chief Mathers was already looking into it but wasn't sure if she could sit still until she said something to him. As she thought about what to say, her phone rang. It was a call from her parents' house.

"Hello?" she answered.

It was an unusual time of day for either of them to call.

"How was the cake I baked you?" her mother asked.

Avery glanced toward the kitchen, where she could see two-thirds of the cake becoming stale.

"It was delicious. Thank you, Mom," she answered.

"Oh, good!" her mom said cheerfully. "I need that plate back, though."

"Sure, Mom, I can swing by tomorrow and bring it if that's okay?" she answered.

"Of course! Any reason to see my darling daughter!" her mother said. "What are you doing?"

"I was just catching up on some stuff," Avery answered.

She was too embarrassed to say she had been snooping into the personal life of a dead man to distract herself from her own intrusive thoughts.

"Well, I'll leave you to it, then," her mother said. "Talk to you tomorrow!"

"Bye, Mom."

"Oh wait, your father says he wants to speak with you."

There was a long pause on the other end of the line followed by the sound of shuffling footsteps.

"Hi, my darling!" her father sang. "What are you up to?"

"Just catching up on some stuff," she repeated. "How are you?"

"I'm good," her father answered. "I just wanted to know if you've put any more thought into this business with Charles."

"Are you talking about the date, Dad?" she asked.

"Yes, that's right."

Avery sighed. "Well, I thought about what you said and decided you were right. It would be completely inappropriate, so I canceled the date."

"That was not what I was suggesting at all!" her father said, surprised.

"What were you suggesting, then?" Avery asked in confusion.

"I meant you should fire him and then go on the date!" her father said with a laugh.

"Dad! I can't do that!" she laughed.

"Why not? I did that with your mother, and it worked," he said.

"Well, you must have been pretty sure about her, then," Avery said. "I can't say that I'm so sure about Charles. Besides, he needs to eat, and this is his income. That would just be cruel."

"So what? If it doesn't work out between the two of you, just hire him back!"

"That would never work," Avery laughed. "It would be too awkward. I figured I'd rather just not take any chances."

"Well, I'm sorry," he said. "How did he take it?"

"I'm not sure, to be honest. We haven't had much time to talk about it. I'm sure we'll get the chance eventually, though."

"Well, I'm sure everything will be just fine," her father said reassuringly. "Things always work out the way they're supposed to."

Her father had always said that, and Avery wasn't sure that she agreed. Often, life simply wasn't fair. Things might have worked out in the end, but she wasn't sure if it was how they were *supposed to.*

"Well, I best be going," her father said. "Listen, your mother wants her cake plate back."

"I know," Avery sighed. "I'll bring it by tomorrow."

"Alright, I'll let her know."

Their conversation ended, and Avery found herself right back where she had been before she had taken her shower. There was no message from Charles yet. Without wanting to look any further into the twisted drama of the Gadling family, she opted instead for a walk.

Chapter Seventeen

It was late in the evening already, and Avery was showing no signs of sleepiness. Unfortunately, she was restless. Her mind kept replaying everything she had read on Oliver and Jack's social media profiles over and over again.

Eventually, she couldn't take it anymore. She typed out an email to Chief Mathers about what she had learned and told him that she felt they made good suspects. Although she was certain he was already aware of them, she knew it would put her mind at ease if she did it.

There had still been no word from Charles. Avery didn't want to check her phone anymore, either. Because every time she learned that there was nothing there from him, her disappointment grew greater.

There were so many worries on her mind. She feared that somehow she would lose the friendship she had with him over it all, although she knew him better than that. There was little logic left in her mind, it seemed.

Avery turned the music on her phone as loud as it could go and began to clean around the house to keep herself busy. It had been some time since her house had been that clean. Every inch was dusted and polished, even the lampshades.

Sprinkles was exhausted from watching it all and had been sleeping most of the afternoon. He also showed no signs of waking up anytime soon, either. Light snores came from his bed, and his legs twitched from his dreams.

A familiar chime echoed through the walls of her home, catching her attention. It was the distinctive sound of a notification on her laptop, indicating the arrival of a new message. She was confident that her inbox was bustling with messages, as she hadn't taken the time to check it in a couple of hours.

But for some reason, that one sounded urgent.

Avery poured herself a glass of merlot and walked toward the laptop. The only thing left for her to clean in the house was her inbox. She slumped down in front of her laptop, preparing her mind for a stream of spam messages.

There were some spam messages and also a few requests for the pond tasting area to be booked for functions. Those were flagged as important.

There was also a response from Chief Mathers, thanking her for her email and assuring her that the men were being looked into. Her eyes glanced over the rest of the emails.

They were the typical ones she saw on a daily basis. She looked at the clock; it was almost midnight. There was no way she would be able to sleep yet, so she got to work tediously unsubscribing from all the nonsense emails.

She was about to close her laptop when a new email came through. It was from Charles. Avery reached for her phone to see if she had missed something. There was nothing.

Why would he email her?

Nerves washed over her as she looked back to her screen. She had been correct. It was from Charles, and the subject line read, "Problem Solved."

Avery hesitantly opened the mail and began reading.

To Avery,

*It is with great excitement that I inform you of my resig-
nation as Wine Room Manager, effective immediately. I
thank you for your kindness and for the opportunity to
work for Le Blanc Cellars, but it is time that I move on.*

*I have accepted an offer to rejoin the Los Robles Police
Force and will be starting with them tomorrow.*

*It is my recommendation that Beth takes over as manager.
I think she is ready and has proven herself to me many
times. I wish you luck in your future business endeavors
and look forward to watching the vineyard's success.*

*Sincerely,
Charles.*

Avery couldn't believe it. She read the words over and over
again, hoping that they would be different. Her hands were
shaking, and her mouth suddenly became parched. A sip of wine
was no help.

She took a deep breath and continued to read, her heart
threatening to leap right out of her chest and onto the keyboard
in front of her.

*P.S. I learned a long time ago that it pays to take risks. Do
not feel bad about this. It is a risk that I am willing to
take. I hope to see you soon.*

Avery leaned back in complete shock at what she had just

read. She took a large gulp of wine and stared blankly at her screen.

There was no sleep for her that night, no matter how hard she tried. Avery would climb into bed and get back out to sit in front of her screen. She would start to type out a response and delete it immediately after.

She did not know the right words to say to him. Avery had read the email at least ten times already, and she had typed out at least twenty different responses. She wasn't happy with any of them.

In fact, she barely knew how to feel about it at all. It was not the response that she had expected from him. She trusted Charles more than anybody else she knew, even so, she didn't know if she really was worth the risk for him.

And she didn't know how to tell him she felt that way.

Instead of typing a response to Charles, she typed out an email to Beth letting her know of her promotion to manager. Charles was supposed to work in the wine room the next day.

The thought of his face not being the one to greet her when she walked in there made her feel sad. But he had made his choice, and she could not tell him what to do. Avery had finally heard from him like she had been hoping to all day.

But it wasn't the response she expected. She felt completely bulldozed by his email to her and had no idea what to do with her emotions. She decided to blame her father for it.

In the morning, Avery had dark bags under her eyes. She did her best to liven herself up with some makeup and by tucking her hair back. But it didn't seem to do anything.

Then with her coffee in hand, she headed toward the police station. She had decided somewhere between three and four a.m. that she would rather speak to Charles in person.

Avery had hoped that the inspiration for what to say would come to her somewhere between then and now. But it hadn't. As she drove to the station, she still had no idea what she wanted to say to him.

There was no way to change the way things had gone, but she still felt poorly. Avery sat for a few minutes outside the station to prepare herself and find her courage. Then, she entered the station.

"Avery," Chief Mathers said with a smile. "Are you alright? It's a surprise seeing you here!"

"Morning," Avery said sleepily. "I'm actually here to see Charles. He resigned last night."

"I fear I might be responsible for that," Chief said, scratching his head. "I've been putting a bit of pressure on him."

Avery chuckled. "I think we share the responsibility here," she teased.

Chief Mathers smiled with a hint of guilt on his face.

"Well, Charles is here," Chief Mathers said. "In uniform and all. But he's in an interrogation at the moment."

"Oh," she said. "That's okay. I'll wait. But I might deplete your stock of coffee." Avery motioned toward the coffee machine that serviced the waiting room.

"You should watch the interrogation," Chief Mathers said. "Charles is fantastic at it. I love to watch him work."

Avery shook her head. "Oh no, no thank you," she said. "Too many people got upset last time."

Chief Mathers winked at her and motioned for an officer to pour her a cup of coffee.

"I won't tell anyone," he said in a low whisper. "Come on, I insist."

Avery took the coffee cup from the officer and followed Chief Mathers to the interrogation room. There they stepped into the room meant for viewing. Neither Charles nor the person in question would know that they were there.

"You know, I'm thrilled that Charles took the job," Chief Mathers said casually. "I'm sorry to have taken him from you. Until yesterday, I wasn't certain he was interested. But he really is going to be an excellent addition to our team."

"I believe he is an excellent detective," Avery said. "Yes, his decision came suddenly, didn't it?"

Avery and the Chief turned their attention to the interrogation, and Avery immediately recognized the man being questioned as Oliver. She had seen enough of his photographs online to know it was him.

"William's brother," she said.

"Yeah," Chief Mathers said. "Charles went to pick him up this morning."

Oliver seemed more than a little displeased to be there. He tapped his fingers impatiently on the table as he waited for Charles to start his questioning.

"Oliver," Charles said. "You're here because your brother was murdered."

"That's no news," Oliver scoffed. "What? Did you think I didn't know?"

"I'm sure you know by now," Charles said. "You're here because of your history with William. We are aware of two court cases between the two of you. It is no secret that you and your brother did not have a good relationship."

"So?" Oliver said. "You think I did it? Don't be ridiculous. I hated the man enough not to want to even get close to him. I wouldn't have done it."

Charles reached to the side and pulled closer a stack of papers, from which he began reading. Avery recognized the words as some of Oliver's social media posts regarding his brother.

"William will get what's coming to him. He will get what he deserves—take my word for it. I will not stop until this is over," Charles read.

Oliver clenched his jaw.

"I wrote that, but that doesn't mean I did it. I was talking about karma, you know?" Oliver argued.

Charles didn't stop.

"My brother does not belong on this Earth. He is scum. He hurts everybody he knows. Soon enough he'll be all alone, spending the money that was meant for me," he read.

Charles continued reading as Oliver argued every word. But Charles did not relent. He read over Oliver's arguments, keeping his tone and volume consistent while ignoring every word that Oliver said.

It was an excellent way to annoy the person in question. Chief Mathers was right. Charles was very good, and his interrogation was a lot of fun to watch.

"Oh, c'mon, man! Just stop it! I get it, okay!" Oliver eventually shouted, slamming his fists on the desk.

"Okay, well, there is one way we can prove your innocence, despite these incriminating words here," Charles said.

"Please tell me," Oliver said sarcastically. "I'd love to get out of here and back to my daily duties."

"Where were you that night?" Charles asked.

"The night he died?" Oliver asked, to which Charles nodded.

Oliver sighed and rubbed his eyes.

"I was doing some late-night shopping. I can't stand mothers and families, so I shop at night. There's a small grocery store that is open twenty-four hours just outside of town. I spent quite a few hours there," Oliver explained.

"I suppose they have cameras we can check?" Charles asked.

"Yeah, and my friend works the counter. He'll confirm seeing me there. We hung out for some time that night," Oliver answered.

It amazed Avery at the notion that a man like Oliver could have a friend. But about thirty minutes later, Charles returned

with a combined alibi. Oliver was asked about any other potential enemies of William. But he no longer wanted to work with
the police.

He got out of there as fast as he could.

Jack was the last one left on the list of suspects.

Chapter Eighteen

The interrogation had come to an end, and Chief Mathers let Avery know Charles was waiting for her in the break room. Avery still had no idea what to say, but it couldn't wait any longer.

Her guilt wouldn't let her sleep, and she needed to do something about that. She paused just outside the door and took the deepest breath she could, releasing it slowly. It had always worked for her before when she needed to calm her nerves.

But it seemed to be of no help at all that day.

Without wanting to keep him waiting, she opened the door and stepped inside. Charles was waiting for her with a wide smile on his face. It put her at ease, but she still did not know what to say to him.

She opened her mouth, hoping that the right words would come tumbling out. But Charles held up his hand to stop her from speaking.

"There is nothing you need to say to me," he said kindly.

"But Charles—"

"But nothing," he said with a smile. "I do not want you to concern yourself with this. This is not your fault."

Avery let out a sigh of relief. "Are you sure? I did not mean for you to go to such extreme lengths. I didn't hear from you at all, and then I got a resignation letter. I just didn't know what to think."

"I know, and I'm sorry," Charles said. "I should have spoken to you sooner, but I got so caught up in everything here."

"You don't have to go to such extremes," Avery said. "I hope you know that."

He replied, a smile gracing his lips. "You know, I had been contemplating it myself. However, I lacked the courage to take the leap. Our conversation served as the catalyst I needed. Instead of blaming you, I should be expressing my gratitude. Thank you, truly."

Avery slumped down in the chair. She felt such relief at that moment. Everything was alright, and all her concern and worries had been for nothing. Her mind had cheated her out of a night of sleep.

"Do you want another cup of coffee?" Charles asked.

"Oh, no thank you," Avery said. "I've had far too much already. One more cup and it might start having a reverse effect."

Charles nodded in agreement. "What about later?"

Avery smiled. "We'll have to do it another day," she said. "I am seeing the Stammtisch women later today."

"I'll take your word for it," Charles laughed.

Avery stood up to leave. "Are you sure you're happy with all of this?" she asked.

"Yes," Charles said without hesitation. "So our date is back on?"

"Yes," Avery answered. "Talk to you later about it."

With that, their conversation came to an end, and any worry Avery had in her mind and heart had been silenced. She felt calm again, but despite that, she would miss Charles around the vineyard.

As she walked out of the precinct, she felt much lighter.

It was a sunny afternoon as the women of the Stammtisch and their dogs went for a walk through the Los Robles gardens. There were rolling lawns and widespread flower gardens all around them.

The park was a place that Avery loved but hadn't visited in some time. Pathways meandered through the park, making loops and detours in every direction. Large trees created shade, and dogs and children played together everywhere.

She had been telling the women about Charles' decision to resign from the vineyard, and all of them were as shocked as she was.

"Did your dad really fire your mom so he could date her?" Eleanor asked.

"Yes," Avery answered. "But let's not forget how many years ago that was. Jobs weren't scarce then. She literally marched into the business next door, and they gave her a job there."

"Still, that's kind of romantic," Deb said. "Just like what Charles has done for you. I think it's very romantic."

"I'm glad you do," Avery chuckled. "And I suppose it is. But it was really stressful. I got so worried about him. Being a detective is dangerous work, and I don't want him to do that just because of me."

"That's what's so romantic about it!" Deb said. "He's willing to risk his life for you."

"I don't think it's romantic," Avery responded. "I'll be so worried. But perhaps I will get used to it, eventually. He's my friend. I don't want to see him get hurt."

The spaces of the park were filled with people out to enjoy the sun. School had ended, and families walked together, just as Avery had done with her parents countless times in her childhood. There were couples that walked together hand-in-hand, enjoying the wonderful weather. There were birds that chirped and sang all around them. It was a brilliant day.

There was a loud splash to the left. Someone's dog had jumped headfirst into the fountain, and its owner had soon followed.

"Food truck!" Tiffany announced, pointing it out. "I need some coffee. Anybody else?"

Most of the women agreed, but it was the first time that Avery didn't join in. She'd had far too much coffee that day and couldn't risk another cup. Besides, she was eager to sleep. If she had another cup, she might not sleep at all again that night.

But she was in a much better mood than when she had woken up. Not only had she spoken to Charles and felt better about that, but the surrounding park was filled with laughter and cheerful conversation.

It would be impossible for anybody to be in a bad mood there. As tired as Avery was, she hoped she could be there for at least another hour or two. If she went home, she'd have nothing to do but focus on her own thoughts, and that was a very dangerous place to be.

"So, what are you guys doing for your date?" Tiffany asked as she sipped her coffee.

"I don't actually know yet," Avery asked. "But I'm sure I'll find out soon enough."

"Don't you want to know? Didn't you ask him?" Tiffany asked.

Avery laughed. "Is that a normal thing to do?" she asked.

"I don't know," Tiffany shrugged. "But I wish I had. If I had known Aaron was going to take me to his own restaurant, I might have suggested something else. I can never go eat there again. And the food is so good!"

Sprinkles bumped up against Avery's leg, and she bent down to pet him on the head. He seemed happy to be at the gardens, and she could already see him gearing up for a long night's sleep.

When Avery looked up again, she noticed a couple walking hand-in-hand up ahead. They stood out because, despite the warm weather, they were completely covered with hoodies, hats, and sunglasses. They certainly stood out from the rest of the crowd.

The first thing Avery wondered was if they were celebrities of some kind. She realized they couldn't possibly be famous. If they were, Deb would have known about it and told the world.

They seemed to walk as if they were a little uncomfortable. Avery watched them getting nearer. When they spotted her looking, they immediately let go of each other's hands.

It was an odd scenario. Something about Avery spotting them had made them very uncomfortable. It only made her watch them even closer. Whoever they were, it was clear to her that they didn't want to be seen together.

Then the woman veered off down another path and away from their group entirely. All Avery really could see was the tip of her blonde ponytail sticking out from beneath her hat.

The fact that she chose to walk away from the man whose hand she'd been holding just a few moments ago struck Avery as very odd. The man still walked toward them, though.

Avery squinted to try and get a look, but she didn't want to seem as if she was staring at him. Their group was talking loudly and laughing, and Sprinkles was walking and jumping merrily at her side.

As they passed the man on the path, he turned his head in the other direction, as if he didn't want them to look at him. Avery grew more and more concerned that something unfriendly was afoot.

It wasn't until she walked right past him that she knew there was something very wrong with the entire scenario. The moment the man passed her, Sprinkles started to cower and whine, as if he was afraid.

She knew that she'd only seen that kind of behavior once before when she had been walking with Marcus.

As she turned back to look, she noted that the man was the right height and build and seemed to walk in a similar fashion. She knew it had to have been Marcus.

But whose hand was he holding? And why the secrecy about it all? Avery thought about the woman he had been walking with and tried to figure out who it might be.

She thought about the morning when she had gone to see Marcus and tried to remember what they had spoken about and why he would try to avoid her in the gardens that day.

That's when she remembered William's wife at the vineyard, and it dawned on her. The woman who had been holding Marcus' hand was William's wife. Avery stopped dead in her tracks and looked back to find him.

But he was long gone, and she couldn't see him at all anymore. The entire thing was making her skin crawl. She didn't like the thought of it one bit. It also put his behavior at the vineyard in perspective.

He had been with her that morning before Avery arrived, which was why he seemed so cheerful and happy, despite what Deb had reported the day before.

By the time Avery got home, Sprinkles was completely exhausted. It was still light out, but he didn't seem to be awake enough to care. He curled up in his bed and went right to sleep without worrying much about dinner.

Of course, her mind was swimming with thoughts of Marcus and Mrs. Gadling together. She couldn't stop thinking about it. How long had they been seeing each other? Avery tried to convince herself that they had simply met after William's death and hit it off.

But she had lost her own husband, and she knew that it simply wasn't possible. She needed a distraction...she didn't want her mind to be so tortured by the thoughts. She needed to switch it off so she could get some sleep.

Avery spotted her notebook on the side table by her couch. It had the list of meals for her dream restaurant in it. It was perfect. She took a seat and lifted the notebook to look through it again.

Naturally, she was in a different mood that night, so she wanted completely different food than what she'd had on that piece of paper. She started drawing lines through the foods she was no longer in the mood for and replaced them with other options that tickled her fancy a little more.

Then she started making notes on the side of the list of wines she could pair it with. She was having fun, and the more wine she added to the food the more food she added to the list.

Eventually, she fell asleep on the couch with the pen in her hand. Sprinkles woke her up a few hours later and prompted her to go to bed. Thankfully, she slept right through the night, her mind and body getting the rest that she needed.

Chapter Nineteen

Avery had eventually given in and phoned Charles. No matter what she did, she could not shake the thought of Marcus and Mrs. Gadling from her mind. Although, she had spoken to Marcus, and he had not given her any reason to believe that he would be having an affair with the victim's wife.

Still, she was convinced by what she had seen in the gardens. Avery was confused and frustrated, and she just wanted to get it off her mind and make it somebody else's problem. Then, maybe, she could stop agonizing over it.

"Everything alright? It's pretty early," Charles said, sounding concerned.

Avery glanced at the clock. He was right. It was just after five o'clock in the morning.

"Sorry," she sighed. "I thought it was a little later than that. Would you like me to call you back later?"

"No, that's alright. You know me. I'm an early bird. What's on your mind?"

"I saw Marcus yesterday at the Los Robles gardens," she explained. "And I'm pretty sure he was walking hand-in-hand with Mrs. Gadling. It was really weird, and it has been bothering me."

There was a brief moment of silence on the other end of the line. Then he responded as if he had only just pieced together what she had said.

"Wait, what?" Charles said. "Are you sure?"

"Yeah," Avery said. "I mean, he had his hood on and some glasses, but I'm pretty sure it was him. Sprinkles does this weird thing where he kind of cowers and whines whenever he's around Marcus. He was doing that yesterday when the man walked past me."

The moment she said it, she heard how strange it sounded.

"That's unusual behavior for Sprinkles," Charles said.

"Yeah," she answered. "It's the only time he's ever done that, which is why I'm certain it was Marcus."

"You said he was with Mrs. Gadling?" Charles said. "As far as we know, the two of them don't even know each other. How can you be so sure it was her?"

"Well, a few days ago I went to see Marcus at his vineyard and check up on him, and when I got there, I passed Mrs. Gadling as she was leaving," Avery explained.

She poured herself a cup of warm coffee while she spoke.

"I thought it was odd for her to be there," Avery continued. "Marcus was really cheerful, too. I mean, the entire reason I was there was because Deb told me he wasn't doing well, and I wanted to check on him."

"I remember you telling me something about that," Charles said. "Go on."

"The woman he was with in the gardens had the same color hair. She had a hat on and some sunglasses, and when she saw us, she veered off in another direction. It was very odd, and I thought she was kind of familiar, but I couldn't quite place her immediately," Avery explained. "It was only a while later that I realized it was Mrs. Gadling."

"That is very strange," Charles said. "You're right to think there's something suspicious there."

"Do you think Mrs. Gadling could be a suspect?" Avery asked. "It's often the spouse."

"We've already looked into her," Charles explained. "She has an alibi, and it checks out."

The knot in Avery's stomach tightened the more they spoke about it.

"I don't like any of this," she admitted out loud.

"Neither do I," Charles said. "Something really isn't right here."

The warm coffee flowed down Avery's throat and did absolutely nothing to soothe her nerves. Her hands were shaking, and she could feel a headache brewing.

"That leaves Marcus," Avery said, stating the obvious.

"Yeah," Charles said. "And we questioned him on the night the body was found and then another time after that."

"And he had an alibi?" Avery asked.

"He was at home in bed. His report from where his house alarm had been switched on and off kind of proved it, but that would be easy enough to do without being there," Charles said. "Chief Mathers is going to love this."

"You better talk with him, then," Avery said.

Their conversation ended, and Avery immediately began pacing the house. Sprinkles walked loyally at her side the entire time. Then once again, she went into autopilot mode. She did her chores and all her work for the day.

She even spoke to her mother and father, but by the time the phone call was over, she had no idea what they had talked about. Avery tried to make herself some lunch, hoping food would soothe her nerves.

Finally, her phone rang, and it was Charles calling her back.

"Hey, Charles," Avery said eagerly.

"You're very good at this, do you know that?" Charles said.

"You were right. We've got evidence to prove that Marcus and Mrs. Gadling have been having an affair for quite some time."

"You're kidding," Avery said.

"I wish I were. We've got multiple videos from cameras in various restaurants showing them together," he said. "And they look pretty close and cuddly."

Avery sat down on the couch, her head spinning. She thought about every time she had been in Marcus' presence. He'd been so friendly and kind and unsuspecting. Her mind flooded with how shocked he had been when the body was found in the wine room.

"I don't believe it," Avery said. "I must admit I was hoping I was wrong."

"Well, I'll tell you something," Charles said. "Sprinkles is an excellent judge of character."

"Wait, what about Jack?" she asked. "William's son. He hates his father and has more motive than anybody else. Just because they're having an affair doesn't mean he did it."

"We questioned Jack already," Charles said. "Let me tell you, that kid is a real brat. I've never met anybody so entitled in my life."

"And? How did the questioning go?"

"He purposefully spoke in circles, clearly impressed by his own ideas and his intelligence," Charles explained. "It wasted a huge amount of my time. But, in the end, he has a sound alibi. It checked out. We have proof he was in a club the night that his father died."

"Oh," Avery said, almost disappointed. "I see."

"We had to let him go even though I didn't want to," Charles continued. "I can't help but think that he is hiding something."

"Hiding something?"

"Yeah, it felt to me that there was something he wasn't telling us," he said. "The kid has been in trouble with the law before, and my guess is that he doesn't trust the police. But he knows something, I am sure of it."

"Marcus has motive now," Avery said.

"We asked him if he knew William and his family, and he told us they'd never met," Charles said. "We now know that it was a lie."

"Yeah," Avery said. "And he obviously has access to the wine cave."

She thought back to her conversation with him from just a few days ago. Something inside her made sense of it all.

"The other day," she said. "When I was talking to him. He was cheerful and chatty, and then when I reminded him about the murder it was like a switch went off with him. I felt guilty at first, and I thought I had ruined his mood, but..."

"But what?" Charles asked.

"But now I am thinking perhaps he had just suddenly remembered how he was supposed to act," Avery said. "I had not ruined his mood. He had just forgotten to be sad."

"You might be right, but let's not get ahead of ourselves here," he responded. "We're going to pick up Marcus now and bring him in. We hope he'll talk after we show him the evidence we have of his affair."

"Will you bring in Mrs. Gadling, too?" Avery asked.

"I'm not sure; I'll have to ask the Chief. But I think Marcus is our prime suspect now," he said.

"Keep me posted," she requested.

"Of course."

Once again, their conversation had ended, and Avery found herself unable to think straight or concentrate on anything. Eventually, she put on a movie to watch, but it didn't work. She was forty minutes into the movie before she realized she hadn't been watching at all.

She'd been staring at a spot on the wall just beyond the television. The only thoughts on her mind had been about Marcus and his behavior. She thought about the body she had found and how distraught Marcus had been.

Then she thought about Deb, who had spoken to him, and he had been shaken up about it all. Enough so that she brought it up in conversation. Avery was so stressed about it all that when she noticed again, she was chewing on her nails.

When her phone rang, she ran through the house to get to it.

"Charles?" she asked.

"Yeah," he answered.

Immediately, Avery could tell that something was wrong. He didn't sound excited, and not enough time had passed for them to have picked him up and taken him in for an interrogation.

"Marcus isn't here," he said. "We've asked around, and he hasn't been seen since yesterday."

"Oh no," Avery said.

"We think that he might have gotten spooked after seeing you in the gardens," Charles explained. "He might have skipped town."

"Now what?"

"We've closed off the roads that leave town, just in case he's still around," Charles said. "And we're going to search for him. But we need to act quickly."

"He's a friendly man," Avery said. "People like him. They'll help him if he asks because they don't know any better. What if he hurts someone else?"

"Chief was thinking the same. We might run his face on the news and list him as an official suspect. Hopefully, somebody knows where he is."

Avery couldn't believe it. It felt as if Marcus had been hiding in plain sight.

"Do you think he'd come after me?" Avery asked. "Since I saw him at the gardens?"

Charles sighed. "I don't think so, but we clearly have the wrong impression of him. I'd rather you be safe than sorry."

"I'm going to go to a friend's house," Avery said, already reaching for her handbag.

"Good idea. The more people, the merrier," he said.

She ended the call, and within forty minutes, Avery and the rest of the Stammtisch were seated in Tiffany's house, watching every window for a sign of Marcus.

Chapter Twenty

The next day, everybody had to go to work, and that included Avery. She spent most of the day worrying Marcus was around every corner or behind every bush, though. It felt like a nightmare.

She had already told Tiffany that she wouldn't spend the next evening there. Avery wanted to be home; she felt safe there most of the time. As evening rolled around, she made triple sure to lock every door and every window.

"This is ridiculous," Avery whispered under her breath. "I shouldn't have to feel this way at home."

Avery had just poured herself a cup of tea when she received a message from Tiffany, telling her to watch the news. She hadn't watched the news in years, and she struggled to find the right channel for it.

But when she found it, she saw Marcus' face plastered all over the screen. The news reporter was asking the community to look out for him and let them know of anybody matching his description.

There was also a small reward for finding him. It wasn't

much, but it was a decent incentive for such a small town. They had told the entire town that Marcus was a suspect in a murder case.

They listed Marcus as a man on the run and as a dangerous man. What followed was a screen capture of some footage of him and Mrs. Gadling together.

"They've really gone all out with this," Avery mumbled.

The news report was barely finished when she heard her phone ringing in the other room. It was Deb, naturally.

"Hi, Deb," Avery answered.

"He's all over the news now!" Deb shrieked. "They really can't find him!"

"I guess they really want to find him," Avery said. "I think it's a good idea. Everyone will be looking out for him. I'm sure he'll be caught soon enough."

"I always knew there was something wrong with him," Deb claimed. "I could see it in his eyes. I thought he was a liar, I just didn't want to say anything because I was worried I was wrong."

"I thought he was pretty honest, actually," Avery said. "He was odd, but I didn't think he had a reason to lie."

"Do you want to know what I think?" Deb asked.

She sounded angry at Marcus, and Avery couldn't help but chuckle a little because of it. Deb was rather comical when she was angry, and Avery could picture her with her hands on her hips as she spoke.

"Tell me," she said.

"I think he took us to that cave because he knew we would find the body," Deb said. "I think he didn't know what to do with it and figured if we found it, then it would be over. He obviously thinks he's a good actor."

"He had us all fooled," Avery said. "You have to admit, he is *kind of* a good actor."

"Well, I feel hurt by him," Deb said. "So much so that I think I want to go out there and look for him."

"Where would you even start?" Avery asked.

"At the gardens, of course," Deb said. "He clearly knows his way around there, and there's plenty of hiding space. It would take the police days to search there."

"Well, don't go alone," Avery said. "If you go, I'm coming with you."

Deb gasped. "Maybe all the girls want to go!" she said excitedly. "Then we can go as a team. Marcus wouldn't stand a chance!"

Avery wasn't so sure about that. But she agreed it would be better to go as a team, and she was tired of being afraid in her own home that Marcus might appear somewhere to get her.

"You can count me in," Avery said.

"How fun!" Deb said. "I'll ask the rest of the ladies if they want to come. I'll let you know, but we'll meet in the gardens. Bring Sprinkles."

"Of course," Avery said.

Deb hung up the call, and Avery wondered if it was the best plan. She thought of how Marcus had killed William. It was a terrible way to die. He had clearly thought the murder through and had been meticulous with it.

She wondered then about what Deb had said about him wanting them to find the body. Avery hadn't even thought about that. It did seem possible, given the amount of thought he'd put into every other detail of the crime. It made Avery's blood turn cold.

Just in case, Avery hopped through the shower and got dressed appropriately for a manhunt. That included sweatpants, a warm hoodie, and some walking shoes. By the time she was out of the shower and ready to leave, she received word from Deb that they were to meet at the gardens in forty minutes.

The rest of the Stammtisch women were going to join them. It seemed that nobody could sleep soundly when there was a murder suspect on the run. Avery had one more cup of tea and then led Sprinkles to the car.

Despite his confusion as to why they were leaving home after dark, Sprinkles seemed excited for whatever adventure lay before him that night. He lay on the back seat and tried to look out the window, but it was too dark for him to see anything.

The nighttime in the town had always seemed so peaceful to Avery. But that night it was different. There was a murder suspect lurking somewhere around there, and she kept envisioning him jumping out from somewhere.

Avery checked her bag for the third time to make sure that the flashlight was there and was relieved when she felt it. There were few streetlights in the town, so it was very dark.

It was a quiet night there as well. Most people had decided to stay indoors until the suspect had been caught, she was sure. That's what her parents would have done, which was precisely why she hadn't told them where she was going.

She was halfway on her way to the garden when she remembered something chilling and important.

Avery pressed the buttons on her steering wheel haphazardly until she finally thought she had the hands-free option working.

"Call Deb," she instructed, wondering if it would work.

To her surprise, she heard a dial tone carry through the speakers of her car. A few seconds later, Deb's excited voice answered.

"Helloooo!"

"Hi, Deb, can you hear me? You're in the car," Avery said.

"I can hear you!" Deb said. "Don't tell me you're not coming."

"No, I am coming," Avery said. "I just think we're looking in the wrong place. Tell the girls to meet me at Marcus' farm."

"They searched his farm," Deb argued. "I highly doubt he's hiding out at home."

"Just trust me," Avery said.

There was some silence on the other end of the line.

"Okay, are you sure?" Deb asked.

"I'm pretty sure," Avery said.

"Alright," Deb sighed. "I'll let them all know."

To Avery's relief, Deb hung up the call. Avery hadn't quite figured out how to do that in the car yet, which was one of the main reasons she hardly used the hands-free option.

She glanced into the rearview mirror and saw Sprinkles fast asleep in the back seat. Avery thought back to the day that she found the body behind the cabinet. It seemed so obvious to her now that Marcus had been behind it.

How could she not have seen it then? Was he really that good of an actor or was he simply not involved? It occurred to her then that he might not have been hiding, and that someone might find him the same way she had found William.

Still, there was something playing on her mind. She remembered the door handle that she had seen sticking out from between the books before she had found the body. Everything else that had happened had caused her to forget about it completely.

What was inside there? Nobody else knew that the handle was there. There was nothing to suggest that whatever was behind that bookshelf was anything important, but it was nagging at Avery.

According to her, hiding in plain sight was the most effective place to remain hidden. His farm was large, and although she was certain the police had checked everywhere, she doubted they had found the handle between the books.

Her car pulled into his vineyard. She was the first person there, and she couldn't help but get a chill as she looked out toward the farmhouse. There were no lights on inside the building, and the vineyard was completely dark.

Avery took a deep breath and then typed a message out to Charles to let him know where they were and what they were doing. It wouldn't surprise her if it upset him, as he surely wouldn't like them putting themselves in that much danger.

She also knew he'd likely arrive at the farm soon after receiving that message.

When she looked up again, she saw Deb and Tiffany arrive in one car. A few minutes later, two more cars arrived, and all the Stammtisch women were together. Avery met them at the entrance to the vineyard.

"What are we doing here?" Deb asked.

"I think I know where he might be, but we need to be careful," Avery explained. "I've let Charles know that we're here, and I'm sure he'll be here any minute to stop us. So, we better get going."

The women nodded in agreement.

"Alright, we must be careful," Avery said. "And we stick together."

Then with Sprinkles and Eleanor's dog at their sides, they started their dark walk through the vineyard. It was pitch black all around them, and their flashlights lit up just enough so that they could see in front of them.

All they could hear was the sound of their feet on the leaves and dirt beneath them. There were no nighttime bugs that sounded. It was as if the entire vineyard had fallen asleep, and they were at risk of waking it up.

Clouds had covered the sky, making it darker than it usually would be. And colder. Avery pulled her shoulders up to warm herself up. All of them walked eagerly and quickly as they searched.

Avery wondered if the other women felt as afraid as she did about it all. She wasn't sure if she was more afraid of searching for him or when she was sitting at home and wondering where he was.

Silently, she cursed Deb for convincing her to do it. She could have been home in a warm bath and then in bed with

Sprinkles at her feet. Instead, they were all there together, doing something wildly reckless.

It almost seemed to Avery that the rest of the women were having fun. It wouldn't surprise her if they were. Searching for a murder suspect seemed just like the kind of pastime that the women of the Stammtisch would be into.

The dogs walked merrily as if they were on some great big adventure. The women walked slowly and carefully, checking down every new row of vines to make sure that he wasn't there, watching them.

It felt very tense to Avery. In the dark, they felt so vulnerable. The women stayed close together, and the dogs stayed around their ankles. Nobody said a word as they walked through the vineyard.

Finally, they made it to the wine cave.

"Here," Avery said. "This is where we need to be."

The women looked at her in complete shock.

"He's not here, Avery," Deb whispered. "The police would have checked!"

"I know," Avery answered. "But I don't think they looked everywhere. Listen, we need to go inside, and we need to switch our flashlights off."

"What?" Tiffany whispered. "Are you crazy? It will be dark. How are we supposed to find him if we can't see him?"

Avery sighed. "The idea is that he doesn't see us first," Avery whispered back. "I'll know if he is near. Trust me. Sprinkles hates him. If Marcus is nearby, Sprinkles will growl."

The women didn't seem to like the idea, but they agreed anyway. Avery turned back to look at the building.

In the dark, with the task at hand, the building loomed over them. Avery reached out, pushed the door, and, to her surprise, it swung open. The women stood for a moment in silence as they looked into the dark space.

Then each of them turned off their flashlights, plunging

them into darkness. Ahead of them lay a large, dark room through which they would have to feel their way.

If Avery was right, somewhere in there was the hiding suspect in a murder case.

"Alright, let's go," Avery said.

Chapter Twenty-One

The room was colder than Avery remembered when she
stepped inside. She looked around her for a moment and
realized she couldn't see a single thing. She couldn't even make
out the outline of the leather couches or bookshelves.

There was no way of knowing how far they'd have to go to
reach the other side or how far to the left she'd have to walk to
get to the place where she had seen the door handle sticking out
from between the books.

Avery started walking first, and the rest of the women
followed hesitantly. None of them knew in which direction to
go or where to search first. So it was silently agreed that they
were cast out like a net, each of them walking in another direction to cover more ground.

The women moved slowly through the dark space. Outside,
it was overcast so they could not rely on any light from the moon
or stars to guide them through it all. By the time Avery was
twenty steps into the room, she'd already knocked several bruises
into her legs.

The other women were doing the same. Each time one of

them bumped something, the rest of them giggled, as if they had forgotten the seriousness of the situation they were in.

It felt like something young teenagers would do to get a scare. Avery could not shake the feeling that they were on the right track, though. Her legs grew weaker with every step as she anticipated finding him there.

The more she thought about Marcus and the way he acted, the more he creeped her out. Yet, there they were, looking for him in the dark. Avery realized at that moment that she hadn't yet thought about what she would do if she actually found him there.

It was too late to be thinking about that. They were there, and they were already more than halfway into the wine cave. She moved carefully past the leather chairs and more or less in the direction that she remembered the shelf to be.

But she could hardly see, so she needed to feel her way through all the spaces.

That was precisely what she did. She felt with her hands across all the books and shelves, searching for the door handle she had seen when she had been there the last time. She slowed her movements with every passing second because she was becoming more and more afraid.

One source of comfort for her was having Sprinkles by her side, walking closely and making his presence known with the gentle brush of his fur against her ankles. The room enveloped them in near silence, with only the faint sounds of the women's cautious movements as they ventured deeper into the darkness.

The deeper into the wine cave they went, the darker it got. As the night air cooled, the building began to settle. Avery jumped with every thump and bump from the settling, thinking it was Marcus somewhere in the darkness.

The other women were getting a fright too. With one particularly loud thump, Deb let out a short yelp. It was followed by a quick and quiet, "Shhh!" from the rest of them.

The women paused briefly and then kept going. Avery's hands felt over books and trinkets and wine bottles, but there was no handle. Had she imagined it? What if she didn't find it? What if it wasn't there?

That thought had not yet crossed her mind. Suddenly, she was concerned about it. If she didn't find it, then she had wasted all their time. The longer she searched, the more likely that scenario seemed to her.

Still, she would not give up until she had checked every shelf in there. So her hands continued to move over the books and trinkets.

Suddenly, she felt something soft to the touch. It was fabric. Then, the fabric moved.

Avery's heart sank. Within a split second, a million thoughts crossed her mind. There was a person there, and she had just touched that person. What if he lunged forward and attacked her? What would she do?

She simply could not run through that dark space. Avery's heart was racing so loud that she could barely hear anything.

"Hey, that's me you're touching," Deb whispered, to Avery's relief.

Avery let out a sigh of relief as the blood came rushing back to the rest of her body again. She felt weak with fear at that moment, and she could feel the adrenaline rushing through her body.

"Sorry," she responded with a light chuckle.

"We've checked the whole place," Deb continued. "I don't think he's here."

Avery closed her eyes and took a deep breath to calm her nerves.

"I'm looking for something," Avery said. "Trust me. I'm sure it's here. And I am pretty sure he's in here somewhere."

"What if we've spooked him and he snuck out?" Deb asked.

"I don't think that happened," Avery responded.

Deb sighed, clearly bored with the situation, and moved away from Avery to keep searching. Avery stopped for a moment to rethink her plan. To search every shelf would take ages. She had to think of something else.

As if her thoughts had been heard, the clouds parted, and the light of the moon and stars filtered through the windows. Somehow, the light coming in made it look even creepier in there. But as Avery's eyes adjusted, she knew she was searching in the wrong place.

She saw the room where she had seen the handle and headed there, motioning for the rest of the women to keep as quiet as possible.

Sprinkles followed her, and he stayed quiet too, as if he knew they were doing something important. She looked at the shelf that she had been searching for and spotted a glint of the metal between the books.

"I found it," she whispered, letting the other women know.

The women stopped and watched as she stuck her hands between the books. Her fingers wrapped around the small handle, and she pushed it down a fraction of an inch.

Click.

It was the sound of a lock opening. With a light push, the shelf in front of her swung open. The books on the shelves stayed exactly as they were as a room opened up in front of her. Avery heard the familiar sound of an empty wine bottle rolling across the floor as she opened the door.

"How did you know that was there?" Deb whispered.

"I saw it when we were here last," Avery said. "Then I forgot about it."

Avery stepped over the threshold with shaking hands and walked into the room. It was even darker in the room than it had been in the wine cave, and there were clearly no windows in there.

Avery pushed past some furniture that had been placed in there and strained her eyes for any sign of a person in there.

"M...Marcus?" she called into the room.

As expected, there was no answer at all.

Avery stood still and listened as carefully as she could, hoping to hear some kind of movement. But when she heard the sound of a light exhale, her blood ran cold.

Then Sprinkles cowered at her side, and a low, guttural growl escaped him. He pressed himself tight against her legs as if to protect her from something that she could not see.

"There's somebody in here," she said loud enough for the women to hear.

The next moment, someone came out of the darkness and pushed her out of the way, running right out of the room.

"Close the front door!" Avery yelled. "He's making a run for it!"

Instinctively, Avery pursued the individual suspected of murder, navigating the room with reckless abandon. In her fervor, she collided with every piece of furniture in her path, but her target was no different. She paid little mind to the obstacles, driven solely by her determination to apprehend him. Fear was not a factor; all she knew was her unwavering desire to capture him.

Marcus ran through a soft beam of light coming from one of the windows, and Avery saw it as her chance. She jumped forward blindly with her arms open. When she felt her arms at his sides, she closed them and gripped him hard.

The velocity of her tackle took them both right over one of the leather couches. Avery and Marcus tumbled down and hit the ground with a loud thud. Marcus groaned as the weight of Avery's body landed on top of him.

Avery's heart was pumping so hard that she barely felt the pain from landing on the ground. All she knew was that she wasn't going to let him go. Marcus struggled beneath her as the women gasped.

"I've got him!" Avery shouted. "Make sure the door is closed and locked. I won't let him get away!"

"Get off of me!" Marcus shouted as he wriggled.

Then he let out a yelp, and Avery felt the softness of Sprinkles at her feet. Sprinkles grabbed the hem of Marcus' pants between his teeth and began tugging. She could hear the sound of the fabric tearing.

Avery couldn't believe it. She had found the murder suspect and was holding him in her arms.

Chapter Twenty-Two

The Stammtisch women ran to Avery and Marcus and turned on their flashlights. When they saw him pinned to the ground beneath her, they cheered loudly, jumping up and down.

Avery was completely out of breath and surprised at her own success with the venture. They all celebrated as if she had caught a large fish or won the lottery.

Marcus had a small trickle of blood running from his nose and over his cheek, and he groaned as the flashlights shone in his eyes. Avery let out a sigh of relief. All the tension of the moments before had melted away, making her weak in the knees.

She was happy she had been able to find him before he found her. That thought had hardly even crossed her mind until that moment. Avery made sure that his arms were tucked beneath her legs as she had learned many years before in a self-defense class.

The women all high-fived each other and rejoiced in their capture of the suspect as if they had just succeeded in a team-building exercise. Marcus could not move. Avery was not a large woman, but she had him pinned down in just the right place so that he could not wriggle free, no matter how hard he tried.

"What is going on?" Marcus asked. "What are all of you doing here?"

"Haven't you seen the news?" Deb laughed. "You're wanted as a suspect in a murder case!"

"He knows that!" Eleanor joined it. "Of course, he knows that!"

Marcus groaned. "Don't be ridiculous," he said. "I didn't do anything. And you're all trespassing."

From where she was, Avery could smell the red wine on his breath, and she could see the redness in his eyes. He had clearly had a lot to drink. He slurred when he spoke, although that could have had something to do with the bump he'd taken to his face when Avery tackled him.

"Why else were you in that small room?" Avery asked. "You're a wanted man, Marcus, and we're your bounty hunters!"

The women cheered again. They had hardly noticed that Charles had arrived on the scene and had walked into the room.

The lights turned on in the wine cave and everyone yelped and jumped, blinded by the brightness of the lights.

"What is going on here?" Charles asked. "I heard you cheering. What—oh."

Charles looked down and saw Marcus with a bloody nose, Avery pinning him down. She flashed him a bright smile. He seemed to be in complete shock when he saw them. He walked closer and knelt down next to Marcus.

"That's our suspect, alright," he said. "Avery, do you think you can hold him down just another minute or two while I call Chief Mathers?"

"I got it!" Avery said proudly as she made herself comfortable.

Charles immediately got on the phone with Chief Mathers

and told him what he had walked into. From where Avery was sitting, she could hear Chief Mathers laughing loudly. Charles couldn't help but chuckle as well.

He then turned to Avery. "I got it from here," he said. "Chief Mathers has asked me to tell you all congratulations."

"Thanks," the women said proudly.

"Are you okay?" Charles asked as he helped Avery up.

"Yeah," she said. "I might be a little bruised, but that's from walking into the furniture."

"Good," Charles said. "I know I don't have to tell you how reckless this was."

"I know," Avery said. "But I didn't have time to convince you all of what I had seen. I figured it would just be simpler to come and look for myself."

"Yeah, but he's a potentially dangerous man," Charles argued.

"Lies!" Marcus shouted drunkenly.

"I said *potentially*," Charles responded.

Within moments, Marcus was under arrest and loaded into Charles' car to be taken back to the station. Avery followed in her car, and the rest of the women followed behind her. They drove as a convoy all the way to the station.

As she drove, Avery felt the tremble in her hands and the nerves in her stomach. They were too late, an afterthought of what she had done. She followed as closely as she could. She just wanted to know that he had made it to the station safely.

But when she got there, she saw that the other women of the Stammtisch pulled into parking spots and followed Charles and Marcus inside. Avery had intended to go back home, but when she saw them enter the station, Avery knew she would have to join them.

She found a spot to park in and walked slowly into the station. The waiting room was filled with the sound of chatter as the women recounted what had happened that night.

"Thank you, ladies," Charles said once Marcus had been taken to have his paperwork filled out. "You ladies can go home now."

"There's no way I'm leaving," Deb said. "I'll never be able to sleep now. I am waiting right here until you come back and tell me what happened."

The rest of the women agreed that they wanted to do the same, and Charles gave up arguing with them about it after the third attempt.

"Can I speak with you?" he asked Avery. "I just need to go over some details."

"Of course," Avery said.

But as she followed him, she saw Deb give her a smile and a wink. Eleanor walked forward and called Sprinkles to follow her back to her seat. Sprinkles was already looking tired and seemed eager for a spot to lie down.

"Have fun, you two," Deb teased.

Avery rolled her eyes. "Sorry about Deb...she sees life as a soap opera."

"Nothing to apologize for," Charles said. "I actually don't need to get any details from you. Deb phoned me on the way to the station and told me everything that happened. I want to ask you if you'll watch the interrogation."

"I don't know if that's the best idea," Avery said.

"You were there on the first day and the last day...I just want you to point out any discrepancies. I want to go through it with him from the beginning and wear him down a little."

Avery shifted uncomfortably.

"Chief Mathers will be there with you," Charles said.

Avery sighed. "Alright, I'll do it," she said.

Charles smiled and guided her toward the viewing room to the side of the interrogation room.

"I'll likely get started in the next ten minutes or so," Charles said. "They should be wrapping up his paperwork soon."

"Okay."

Charles left and barely a minute later, Chief Mathers walked into the room. He had an amused smirk on his face.

"I saw Marcus' face when he walked in here," Chief Mathers said. "Nice tackle!"

Avery blushed and lowered her head. "Thanks," she said with a soft laugh.

They laughed about it for a few moments before the door to the interrogation room opened.

"I guess they were done faster than expected," Avery mumbled.

Marcus was walked in with a bandage over his nose. It was swollen and looked pretty sore. Avery felt a little bad. After all, it could still turn out that he was innocent. Charles walked in soon afterward and sat down in front of Marcus.

"Okay, well," Charles started. "We've been looking for you. In the end, you were hiding in plain sight."

"I wasn't hiding," Marcus said miserably.

"What were you doing in that room, then?" Charles asked. "We have officers over there now. They say there isn't much in there. There's a chair and a table and not even a window. You can't tell me it's a good spot just to enjoy a few bottles of wine."

Marcus clenched his jaw and said nothing. He looked away from Charles and cast his gaze instead on the far wall.

Charles asked a few more questions, all of which were met with silence.

"Perhaps these will help you talk," Charles said, reaching for a nearby folder.

He pulled out three photographs. They were the captures from the security footage of Marcus and Mrs. Gadling together.

Marcus looked at them and went pale.

"Do you think there's something you might want to tell me now?" Charles said, looking pleased with himself.

Marcus nodded. "I want my lawyer."

Chief Mathers let out a frustrated sigh.

"That's it," Chief Mathers said. "We can do nothing until he has his lawyer present."

"That's frustrating," Avery said.

Charles smiled, packed up his files and ledgers, and walked out of the interrogation room, slamming the door closed behind him. Avery went to meet Charles in the hallway, and he looked completely defeated.

"That did not go well," Charles said.

As they walked, Marcus was led from the interrogation room toward the cells. As he saw Charles in the hallway, he started shouting in a drunken ramble.

"I'll take you to court!" he shouted. "For defamation of character. You put my face all over everything. I'm ruined!"

"This guy is annoying," Charles complained.

"I am sorry it didn't go as well as you'd hoped it would," Avery said kindly. "I think you were doing everything well."

"Thanks, but if we must wait for his lawyer, it will take considerably more time for us to end this case," Charles said. "Until then, we simply have to wait and hope that we find some evidence on his property."

"I'm sure everything will turn out fine," Avery said hopefully.

"How did you know about the hidden room?" Charles asked.

"I saw it the day when I found William," Avery explained. "But with the whole ordeal after finding the body, it kind of slipped my mind. It was only when we talked about going to find him that I thought about it again."

When they got back to the waiting room, all the women got to their feet, eager to hear about what had happened. They waited, with hot cups of tea in their hands, for Charles to tell them that Marcus had confessed.

"Sorry, ladies," Charles said. "He asked for his lawyer. That's the end of it for today."

There was a collective sigh of disappointment between them.

"Really?" Deb asked. "How boring."

Charles laughed. "Most police work is boring."

"Okay, well then I guess let's all head home, and we can talk again tomorrow?" Deb said.

The women agreed and were about to head to the door when a young man walked in. Avery immediately recognized him as the son of the victim. Only he didn't look like he did in his photographs.

He wasn't wearing his flashy clothes and expensive accessories. Instead, he appeared to be in pajamas, and, by the looks of it, he had been in those pajamas for a few days.

"Jack, what can we do for you?" Charles said, greeting the man with a kind smile.

"There's something I want to tell you about my father," Jack answered.

It stopped all the women in their tracks, and they all took their seats again, turning their ears toward the conversation.

"Of course, why don't we step into the other room, and we can talk," Charles said.

"Oh, no," Jack responded. "If you don't mind, I'll do it out here. I'm not too comfortable in stations like this, and I'd much prefer it this way."

Charles was reluctant, but he agreed. He was eager for a break in the case, and if Jack had anything to offer, he was going to gladly accept it.

"There was something," Jack said. "And I had forgotten about it completely. But then, when I saw Marcus' face all over the news and heard about his relationship with my mother, I started to think...and I remembered something."

Charles looked at him closely, as if to inspect whether or not the man was telling a lie. But Jack looked pale and concerned, and it was clear to anybody in the room that there was something really bothering him.

"I think you might be onto something with him as a suspect," Jack continued.

"Well, in that case, I have good news for you. We have him in custody," Charles said.

Jack seemed to be relieved. It looked to Avery as if he had been worried about his own safety. There was clearly something up, and Jack knew important information. Avery could feel it in her gut.

Chapter Twenty-Three

Jack was trembling slightly as he tried to tell them what was on his mind. Charles had offered him a seat, but when Jack saw the group of women who occupied the seating area, he politely declined.

"So, what's on your mind, Jack?" Charles asked.

"It's a phone call I got from my father a little while back," Jack explained. "He had phoned me from a blocked number. I had applied for a new job, and I thought it was them calling me to give me some news."

Jack took a deep breath and leaned on the counter next to him.

"He started talking really fast and telling me that he was worried and feared for his life," Jack continued. "He kept saying he didn't have long left and that he just didn't feel right about anything anymore."

There was a startled silence in the room.

"This is so much better than TV," Deb whispered in the background.

"I mean, he sounded pretty upset and stressed out when he

said it, but I didn't give him much time to talk. We weren't on good terms, and I just ended the call."

Avery could see the regret in Jack's eyes. It showed in the way he blinked back tears and swallowed hard after every sentence. There was remorse there, and she pitied him for it.

"Listen, Jack, did this not seem important when we were questioning you about your father's death not too long ago?" Charles asked.

It was a good question. He had not mentioned it before, so why now?

"Look, my father and I didn't talk often," Jack explained. "Sometimes, he would come up with these big, elaborate schemes to get me to call him. He knew that if he could make me worry about him, then I would get in contact."

Charles nodded to say that he understood.

"He'd often tell me he was sick or that he needed help with something. Then I would contact him and it wouldn't be entirely the truth," Jack explained. "One time he even told me that the house was on fire, but it had only been one notebook on which he had accidentally dropped some cigarette ash."

"I see," Charles said.

"Yeah, so I figured this was another one of his ploys to get me to talk to him," Jack continued. "In fact, I thought it was such a feeble attempt that it made me really angry. I don't like to joke about death, and I thought he was being callous and unkind when he said it."

It surprised Avery at what an intelligent man Jack turned out to be in person. His online persona and Charles' experience with him seemed to be so vastly different.

"In fact, I sent him a pretty nasty message afterward to tell him exactly what I thought about it all," Jack said. "When I think about it now, though, it is a haunting thought."

"There was nothing you could have done," Charles said.

"Given your history, you did what you thought was right. That is not a crime."

"But about a week later, he left me a voice message, this time from his own number," Jack continued to explain. "It was one of the strangest voice messages he had ever left me. In fact, I almost texted my mom to tell her to give him a drug test because of it."

"Do you still have the voice message?" Charles asked.

Jack nodded. "Yeah, it's on my computer at home. I managed to get the phone company to send me a recording of it."

"Good!" Charles said. "But what did it say?"

"My dad sounded drunk, and he kept rambling on about how he suspected that my mother had done something with his will and his life insurance policies and stuff," Jack explained. "He said it was ominous and that he had a bad feeling about it."

It was as if the entire case had unraveled in front of them. Told to them like something from a storybook by a man already in his pajamas.

"I didn't respond," Jack said. "My father was not a stupid man. I knew that if it really was a problem, he would simply refuse the increase and would move on from it. I just figured it was another attempt at manipulating me to get in contact with him."

Charles had been writing everything down. There wasn't a single person within earshot that wasn't completely invested in what Jack had to say at that moment.

"Do you know if the policy was changed?" Charles asked. "Do you have any proof that the life insurance on your father had been increased?"

"It was," Jack answered. "By a fairly substantial amount."

"This is really good stuff," Charles said.

Jack didn't look proud or pleased. It was obvious that he wouldn't be. His father had been murdered, and he had been warned about it. Only he hadn't taken that warning seriously. Avery couldn't imagine how terrible that must have felt.

"My father had suspected my mother of having an affair for some time," Jack said. "But he could never get any proof. He was just too busy with work. When it came to my father, work always came first."

"Did he ever mention who he thought she was having an affair with?" Charles asked.

"I would have been surprised if my father knew the names of any of my mother's friends," Jack said. "I've had the same best friend for twenty years, and I don't think my father knows his last name. He wasn't attentive like that. I don't think he knew who the affair was with, I think he just knew that there was an affair."

"Did he tell you that?" Charles asked.

"He offered to pay me to follow my own mother," Jack scoffed. "He wanted me to be his little private investigator. I refused, of course. And I told my mother about it."

"I'm sure that must have upset her," Charles said.

Jack laughed. "There was hardly a day when the two of them weren't upset with each other. Still, I did like to believe there was some love there."

The more that Avery was learning about the Gadling family, the more dysfunctional they seemed to her. She thought of her own family and how different things were for her and her parents. It was like two completely different worlds.

"Thank you for telling us this, Jack," Charles said kindly. "I am sure that this will be what we need to crack this case wide open."

"I just feel so guilty for not listening," Jack said. "He was telling me clearly that he feared for his life, and I didn't take him seriously. I don't think I can ever forgive myself for that."

"Nobody holds you responsible," Avery said, not that it was her place. But she felt bad for him. "Sometimes bad things just happen. The grieving will never end, but you cannot allow your-self to get stuck because of guilt. It cannot be changed, but you will learn to let it go."

Charles looked at her with an impressed look on his face. Which, in turn, made Avery feel slightly embarrassed.

"When I saw on the news that there had been evidence of my mother having an affair, I knew immediately that my father had not been lying when he said he feared for his life."

Charles reached over the counter and poured Jack a glass of water, which the man gladly accepted. He really seemed far more put together than what could be seen on his social media profile. Avery wondered if his uncle was the same. She doubted it.

"You said you have Marcus under arrest?" Jack asked.

"We do," Charles said. "In fact, these are the ladies who helped us catch him."

Charles motioned to the Stammtisch women who had all been watching Jack's story unfold like a theater production that had been put on just for them. When Jack looked over to them, they all waved excitedly with wide smiles.

"Thanks," Jack said sheepishly. "Has he confessed to the murder?"

Charles shook his head. "I'm afraid not. He got wise and lawyered up."

"Chicken," Camille mumbled under her breath, silently shocking everyone in the room.

"That's a pity," Jack said.

There looked to be a heavy weight on Jack's shoulders. He leaned against the table, deep in thought, and Avery wondered if there wasn't perhaps more to his story that he still needed to piece together.

It seemed ironic that a man she had listed as a strong suspect mere days before had so quickly become an integral part of solving the case and putting the real killer behind bars. She made a mental note never to judge someone according to their social media profiles again.

If she thought about it and looked at hers, people would think she disappeared off the Earth months ago. She had stopped posting when she got to the farm.

Jack scrunched his face up as if he had just thought of something.

"Do you think he'll crack if you give him some bad news?" Jack asked. "You know, like if you make him think things haven't gone according to his plan. Would that do the trick?"

Charles tapped his finger on the counter. "I've seen it happen before, but unfortunately, I can't ask him any more questions until his lawyer arrives."

"But you can tell him facts?" Jack asked. "There's nothing that stops you from going in there and just telling him bits of information?"

Charles narrowed his eyes. "What are you getting at, Jack? If you know something more, I suggest you tell me now."

Jack went quiet as if he was trying to decide how much he should say. He looked around the room at all the expectant faces. On the screen above his head, the news banner had changed to let the people of Los Robles know Marcus had been found and arrested.

"I think I might have some news that Marcus would find upsetting," Jack said. "Because I think he did it. I don't think it was my mother. She doesn't care enough about people to murder them. But I think he might have done it if he thought he could get my mother and her life insurance payout."

Charles smiled. "This is turning out to be an interesting evening is it not?" he asked nobody in particular.

"All we need now is some popcorn," Deb teased. "Or some wine."

"I got a call this morning from the life insurance company that has my father's policy," Jack explained. "They've decided to launch an investigation into me because of me being listed as a suspect and his murder and everything."

"That's terrible," Avery said.

"Well, get this," Jack continued. "They say that I'm a suspicious character because even though the policy had always been set to pay out to my mother, it had suddenly been changed to pay out to me."

"That does make you look bad," Charles said seriously.

"It gets worse," Jack confessed. "The change was made mere days before my father was murdered."

Charles smiled. "You think that if Marcus hears there will be no money, he will be upset enough to break?" he asked. "There has to be more to this than just the money. I don't think we'll get him that easily."

"You don't understand how much my mother increased the policy," Jack said with a smile. "It's supposed to pay out well over a million dollars."

Everyone in the room stared at him in disbelief.

"We're not talking about a small sum of money here," Jack said. "I bet Marcus knows exactly how much that policy is worth. He's losing a lot, and so is my mother."

"That does change things somewhat," Charles said with a smirk.

"I think you should bring my mother in, too," Jack said. "Even though I don't think she murdered him, I find it hard to believe that she didn't know anything about it at all."

Chapter Twenty-Four

Charles immediately arranged for Mrs. Gadling to be brought to the police station. Jack was given tea and food while he waited nervously to see his mother be walked through the door.

"What's this all about?" she asked as she was rushed through the door. "Jack? What are you doing here? Are you alright?"

"Hi, Mom," Jack said with a pale face.

Mrs. Gadling looked confused and shocked to see her son there. She had clearly been taken by surprise as she was also in her pajamas. She looked far less glamorous than she had on the other occasions that Avery had seen her.

When Mrs. Gadling saw Avery standing there, there was a hint of recognition in her eyes and she stopped asking questions. Avery wondered if she recognized her from that day in the gardens and knew that she was there to be questioned about the affair.

The Stammtisch women were all whispering among themselves as they tried to come up with their own theories as to what had happened and who was and wasn't guilty. It was as if they were playing a game.

Charles didn't seem to mind too much. He had drowned them out and was simply happy they weren't asking him questions or interfering too much with his job. They all waited as Mrs. Gadling was taken to do some paperwork.

"Listen, Jack," Charles said. "Do you think you could watch the questioning? It will be from a secret room. I only want you to listen in and let me know if someone is telling a lie. It will surely speed up the process."

Jack looked immediately uncomfortable.

"As I said before. Police officers make me a little uncomfortable," he said. "It's no offense, just a bad experience once."

Charles thought it all through for a moment and then looked at Avery and smiled.

"Tell you what," he said. "Avery will be there with you. That way you're not alone in there with a cop."

Avery looked wide-eyed at Charles.

"I think I know who you are," Jack said. "You are the woman who found my father's body."

Avery nodded silently. For reasons she didn't quite understand, that truth made her feel guilty.

"That means you're also the woman who wrote those crime novels, right?" Jack asked. "I've read them all. They're very good."

"My name is Avery," she said, extending her hand. "It's a pleasure to meet you."

Jack smiled and shook her hand. "If she's with me, I might be able to do it. But can I leave if I don't want to be there anymore?"

"We have not detained you," Charles explained. "You can leave any time you want."

Jack mulled it over for some time as he tapped his fingers against the counter.

"Alright," he said. "How will I tell you if they're lying?"

"There is a button in the viewing room," Charles said. "When you press it, a light will go off behind Marcus where he cannot see it. Then I will know that he, or your mother, has told a lie."

Jack nodded. "Let's get it over with then."

Avery and Jack followed Charles back to the viewing room. Just as they disappeared around the corner, Avery heard Deb whisper, "Lucky."

Chief Mathers was waiting in the room. He seemed to be stressed but happy to see Avery and Jack there.

"Another officer told me what you had to say," Chief Mathers said to Jack. "I think it is very cool of you to let us know. Thank you."

Jack gave Chief Mathers a curt nod. "No problem," he said dryly.

Avery positioned herself between Jack and Chief Mathers just as Mrs. Gadling was led into the room with Marcus. She looked at Marcus and immediately went to his side, taking his hand.

Jack let out a loud sigh, and when Avery glanced up at him she saw him clench his jaw. She understood that it must have been uncomfortable for Jack to see his mother with the man she'd been cheating on his father with.

"We've decided to bring you in tonight, Mrs. Gadling because some information has come to our attention, and we'd just like to confirm some facts with you," Charles said.

"He cannot ask Marcus any questions," Chief Mathers commented. "But he can ask your mom. He can speak to Marcus to tell him about any facts. This is going to be tricky for Charles to navigate."

"I'm sure he'll be just fine," Avery said.

"Okay," Mrs. Gadling answered nervously.

"I want to talk about the changes to your husband's life insurance policy," Charles said. "It has come to my attention that just days before your husband's murder, the beneficiary had been changed."

Marcus looked as if all the color had drained from his face.

"The sole beneficiary of that money is your son, Jack," Charles continued. "Is that correct, Mrs. Gadling?"

While Marcus looked completely bowled over by the news, Mrs. Gadling didn't seem moved at all.

"That is correct," she said. "I already knew about that. I am the one who changed it."

It was not the response that any of them had expected. Avery, Jack, and Chief Mathers all glanced at each other. It seemed that they were all at a loss for words. Marcus stared at her as if she had done the worst betrayal he had ever seen.

"I see," Charles said, making notes.

Jack stared at his mother in disbelief.

"I thought my father had done it," he said. "This makes no sense to me."

Avery noted that Marcus had let go of Mrs. Gadling's hand. She didn't seem too concerned about it. She waited patiently for Charles to continue with his line of questioning. Marcus, on the other hand, looked more nervous than he had been before.

His hands fidgeted with each other beneath the table.

"Something doesn't add up here," Jack said.

"I have to agree with you there," Chief Mathers chuckled.

"May I ask you why you made the change?" Charles asked, continuing with his questioning of Mrs. Gadling.

Mrs. Gadling shrugged. "I did it for my son," she answered. "Obviously, I had expected my husband to live many more years than he did. I figured he'd be an old man when he died, and I wouldn't need that money. I'd be old by then too."

With every word out of her mouth, Marcus became more agitated.

"My husband and my son were not on good terms," Mrs.

Gadling continued. "I felt bad about it. I thought that by the time my husband died, my son would be older and better with money. And that he could probably put it to better use than me."

Avery looked at Jack, and it looked as if Jack was going to fall over from surprise. His mouth actually dropped open.

"That's very thoughtful of you," Charles said.

"I wanted to make sure he was protected should something happen to my husband," she answered. "But I assure you, I had nothing to do with his death. I believe I was cleared as a suspect on account of my alibi."

Charles nodded. "Yes, that's correct. I merely want to make sure that I have my information correct."

Mrs. Gadling smiled. "Of course, and I'll do anything to help clear Marcus' name, too."

It looked as if Marcus was no longer listening to anything at all. He stared blankly ahead as if disappointed in how things had turned out in the end.

"Mrs. Gadling, can you think of anybody that might have known about some changes to the policy?" Charles asked.

She went quiet for a moment. "I assume you aren't talking about the change in beneficiary anymore, are you?"

Charles shook his head. "I am referring to the increase in the policy amount. I'm sure you know that his life insurance payout is a rather sizable sum of money."

"Yes, indeed," she responded. "I decided to increase it around the same time I began contemplating passing it down to my son. I never supported the idea of severing Jack's access to our wealth, but unfortunately, I had no say in the matter. This was the only avenue I could think of to ensure he received what I believed was rightfully his. Of course, I understood it would require a long-term approach."

"That's very thoughtful of you," Charles said. "But did you *tell* anybody about it?"

Mrs. Gadling leaned back in her chair, biting her bottom lip as she thought about it for a moment.

"I didn't tell anyone," she said. "But it was lying on my desk for some time. I got distracted while working on the paperwork."

"Was there anyone in the house that could have seen it on your desk?" Charles asked.

"The only other person there was Marcus," she confessed. "He was the distraction."

Jack sank his head into his hands as he listened in on the conversation. Avery couldn't imagine how difficult it must have been for him to hear it all.

Before Charles could ask his next question, an officer knocked on the door and let himself in.

"Pardon the intrusion," the officer said. "But I have something I think you might want to take a look at."

Charles looked up and ushered the officer inside.

"We found this while searching the suspect's house," the officer explained. "It was wedged between the mattress and the bed."

Charles reached out and took a notebook from the officer, paging through it. Whatever was written in there, it made Charles turn red in the face and his eyes shot up at Marcus.

"Mrs. Gadling, I am going to ask you to take a look at this and tell me what you think about it," Charles said. "If you don't mind, could you read it out loud for me?"

She took the book from Charles with a confused look on her face and began to read.

"Policy," she started. It quickly became clear that it was a list.

"Um, policy," she read again. "Water...clean...body found...ring."

She dropped the book in front of her on the table.

"What is this supposed to be?" she asked.

"I believe that is Marcus' handwriting?" Charles asked.

"It is," she said. "He writes me letters, so I know it well. But I don't know what this is supposed to be."

Charles smiled. "I suppose now is a good time to tell you that your husband's lungs were found filled with water," he said. "And that his body was found to be pristinely cleaned."

Mrs. Gadling looked as if the world had come crashing down around her. She stared at the page in front of her as all the pieces fell into place.

"This one here is interesting," Charles said, tapping on the page. "Here where you wrote, *body found*, Marcus. I have been wondering why you chose to give a tour that day. You rarely give tours like that."

"What are you saying?" Mrs. Gadling asked.

Marcus remained quiet, not saying a word.

"I'm saying that it is entirely possible that Marcus led those women there that day, hoping they would find his body. Did you not find it strange that the body of your husband was found in your lover's vineyard?"

Mrs. Gadling burst into tears. "No," she cried. "There has to be another explanation. Of course, it was strange, but strange things happen all the time."

"This list...it shows that it had been carefully planned," Charles said.

He picked up the book and paged through the rest of it.

"Every other page is empty," Charles said. "This is all that's in here. And it was hidden away with the idea that nobody would find it."

Mrs. Gadling moved to the corner of the room where she dabbed at the tears in her eyes. Jack shifted uncomfortably at Avery's side.

"The last one has me most intrigued," Charles said. "*Ring*. I suspect Marcus wanted to marry you."

When Mrs. Gadling turned around again, she had nothing but anger in her eyes.

"You could have just told me," she growled at Marcus. "I could have divorced him. We could have done this like normal people!"

Marcus was hanging on by a thread, and her anger toward him had finally caused him to break. He would get no money, and he would get no wife. Marcus had failed, and the pressure of it was mounting, making him seem defeated.

"How could I have asked that of you?" Marcus broke his silence. "Do you remember who he was? And what he used to get away with? He would use the law to destroy me. If you divorced him, he would have left you with nothing!"

"What does that matter?" Mrs. Gadling snapped. "I might not have had his money anymore, but was I not enough for you?"

Marcus clenched his jaw. It was clear that he didn't want to answer those questions. Charles, on the other hand, sat back and let everything unfurl before him.

"You can't be serious," Mrs. Gadling said, sounding broken. "Please, Marcus, tell me that you weren't with me for the money. Tell me those things you would whisper to me when we were together...tell me that they were all true."

Avery's heart broke as she watched Mrs. Gadling beg her lover for some honesty. She had lost everything. Her husband was dead, and she would likely lose Marcus too. It was difficult not to feel sympathy for her.

"I did it for you," Marcus said as if he had forgotten that Charles was in the room.

"What?" Mrs. Gadling whispered through tears.

"I just wanted to be by your side," he confessed. "I had even selected a ring, believing it was the only way to express my intentions. While the financial support would have been beneficial, my primary motivation was having you exclusively for myself. I had grown weary of sharing."

There was a stunned silence throughout the entire precinct at the suddenness of his confession.

"I knew that divorce would ruin you," Marcus said. "That was not something I wanted for you. I reasoned it would be best if he died. Then we could spend time together without him interfering. Wouldn't you want that as well?"

"Why would I want that, Marcus?" Mrs. Gadling asked with disgust. "I'd have chosen you if you asked. My son has lost a father because of you. Our hearts are broken. How dare you say that you did it out of love?"

With that, Marcus was placed in cuffs and arrested for the murder of William Gadling. By the time Avery turned to check on Jack, he had already left to be at his mother's side.

"We better give them some time," Chief Mathers said. "They've got a long few months ahead of them."

Chapter Twenty-Five

"I'd like to thank you all for your help in catching a killer," Chief Mathers said to the Stammtisch women who filled the waiting room. "When we asked the community to help us keep a lookout for him, we certainly did not expect anybody to go to such extremes. However, we are very grateful."

The women cheered, pleased with the outcome of the day.

"And I must ask each of you never to do that again," Chief Mathers said with a laugh.

"Yeah, yeah," Eleanor said. "It's dangerous. We get it already."

The women giggled at her teasing response. Everybody was tired and ready to go home at that point. Sprinkles had fallen asleep beneath one of the benches.

"I'm also happy to let you know that Marcus is busy giving a full confession as we speak," he said.

Again, the women cheered and high-fived each other.

"However," he continued, more sternly. "I ask that you not divulge this information until it is on the news. Out of respect for the victim's family."

Chief Mathers was looking directly at Deb as he spoke the

words. She nodded, but Avery could see she wasn't pleased with the agreement, and she wondered how long it would stand.

At that moment, Mrs. Gadling passed them on her way to splash her face in the ladies' room. Her eyes were puffy and red.

"Mrs. Gadling," Avery called, going after her. "I hope you don't mind me stopping you for a moment. Those women back there are my friends, and we get together from time to time. It sounds odd, but I lost my husband a while back, and these ladies have been a real support for me."

Mrs. Gadling looked back at the women and then back at Avery.

"I'm sorry for your loss," she said, unamused.

"I'd like to invite you to join us at one of our next gatherings," Avery said. "No pressure, just think about it."

Mrs. Gadling looked as if she might cry again. She forced a small smile and nodded at Avery.

"Thanks," she said. "I'll think about it."

With that, she let Mrs. Gadling go on with her evening and herded the rest of the Stammtisch women out of the door.

Avery pulled on the handle of her car door, eager to get home now that it was all done.

"Avery!" Charles called. "Wait a second!"

She stopped and turned to see him running down the stairs in her direction.

"What's up?" she asked.

Charles smiled. "I'll pick you up tomorrow at six," he said. "For our date?"

"Sure," Avery said cheerfully. "Wait, six in the evening, right?"

"See you," Charles said with a boyish chuckle.

Then he spun on his heels and headed back into the precinct. As much as Avery had hoped they hadn't, the rest of the women had heard him make the arrangements. Part of her felt Charles had done it on purpose to make her blush.

Avery rushed into the driver's seat of her car to block out the sounds of the women teasing her. She closed her eyes and took a deep breath. It had been a wild, emotional day, and she was eager to get into bed.

She drove slowly on the quiet, dark roads home. The rest of the town seemed so peaceful compared to what she had just witnessed. While Los Robles slept and relaxed, Mrs. Gadling had her entire world ripped out from underneath her.

It twisted Avery's stomach into a knot. She knew the loss that Mrs. Gadling was experiencing and couldn't imagine how magnified it would be to learn that someone who loved her had killed her husband.

She was grateful for her simple life at that moment.

Avery pulled up in front of her house. Sprinkles hopped out of the back seat and sauntered over to the door. It wasn't long before Avery was tucked in bed with Sprinkles at her feet.

She reached for her phone and typed out a message to Charles.

Good luck for tonight.

She knew he likely had a long night ahead of him. Avery would ask him about it the next day. She was just dozing off when she heard her phone notify her of an incoming message. It was a response from Charles.

I'll be fine. Excited for tomorrow. Dress warm.

Avery could no longer think about anything. Her mind had been stretched and so had her energy. As she rolled over, she felt her muscles aching from chasing Marcus and tackling him to the ground.

She wondered how she might feel the next day. Thankfully, she had no reason to be up early and intended on sleeping in if her body would allow it. And if Sprinkles would allow it.

She pulled the covers up to her neck and felt the weight of them over her body, imagining that they were a tight embrace. Then she closed her eyes and did her best to think about nothing.

It wasn't long before she and Sprinkles were in a deep sleep, and by the time they woke up, it was already mid-morning. As expected, her muscles ached greatly.

Charles had picked Avery up in a cab at precisely six. Judging by the cab, she figured there would be alcohol involved at some point in the evening. Although it was nothing new for her and Charles to share a bottle of wine between them, somehow that day it made her feel nervous.

He had insisted that he wouldn't tell her where they were going. She had allowed it, but she had never liked surprises. She wore the most makeup she had worn in quite some time. As he complimented her on it, she found herself worried she had over-done it.

Avery didn't know why she was so nervous, either. She had known Charles for some time, and they had been very close friends. It should have been the easiest date in the world. But it wasn't.

It had been so long since she'd been on an official date that she no longer knew what the expectations would be. That was the part that made her the most nervous. Still, every time Charles cracked another joke, she felt more at ease.

Eventually, the cab pulled up outside a building that she recognized immediately.

The Los Robles Zoo.

"I thought this might be fun," Charles said with a smile.

Avery's nerves melted away. "This is really cool!" she said, excitedly getting out of the car. "But aren't they closed by now?"

Charles shrugged. "I know the owner, and he owes me a favor that I haven't cashed in yet. He's given me after-hours access so we can have the place to ourselves."

"You're kidding," Avery said, her heart fluttering in her chest. "Double cool!"

They walked through the zoo as the sun began to set. It was peaceful to see the animals go through the end of their day. Soon, the nocturnal animals would make their appearance.

It was like magic to Avery to have the zoo to themselves. It had a different atmosphere without the hundreds of families and children around. The animals seemed calmer, and the air was fresh.

It was a grand gesture, she realized. And that made her nerves come back to her at full force. To Avery, it was too much for someone to do for her. She figured they'd do something basic like go to dinner or the movies.

Instead, he had arranged a private trip to the zoo for her.

"I have to admit," she eventually said, "you organized one impressive first date."

Charles smiled widely. "It isn't over yet," he teased, nudging her with his elbow.

Avery didn't know what he meant by that, and she chuckled nervously.

"Take it easy, Avery," Charles joked. "I only want to spend some time with you alone and get to know even more about you. The only thing you need to worry about is the potentially deep questions that I might ask you."

Despite never having considered it, Avery realized that if there was anyone in the world she'd be comfortable answering deep questions with, it would be Charles.

Over the next hour, they spoke easily about almost every topic. Charles gave her a rundown of all his past girlfriends.

Most of them had been terrible, except for one that Avery learned had passed away.

It had saddened her, but he assured her he was alright and that he had healed from it. Avery told him about her husband, and he did not run away. Instead, he made an effort to learn about him and the life they had shared.

They laughed and teased each other relentlessly as they walked through the endless animal enclosures.

"Can I ask you something?" Avery asked.

"Of course," Charles teased. "Isn't that kind of what we're doing here?"

Avery nudged him. "When exactly did you decide that you wanted to take me on a date?" she asked.

"Did it take you by surprise when I asked?" Charles responded.

"A little," she answered honestly. "But you can't avoid my question by asking another question, Mr. Police Officer."

Charles gave a nervous chuckle.

"You want the honest truth? Or the answer that makes me feel less foolish?" Charles said.

"Honest truth," Avery said with a sassy smile.

"The first day that we met," Charles said. "But of course, that would have been wildly inappropriate, and I barely knew you then."

His answer had not been what she expected to hear.

"If I'm even more honest," he continued, "I had hoped that the feeling would fade the more I got to know you. But it didn't, I guess. Now, here we are."

Avery wasn't sure if it was the setting sun or not, but it seemed almost to her as if Charles was blushing. She didn't know what to say to him anymore. They walked quietly for a moment.

"I hope I didn't make things awkward now," Charles said with a laugh.

"Not at all," Avery said. "I guess, I just don't know how to be on a first date."

"You're doing a good job," Charles cheered her on.

They turned a corner, and Avery gasped. Ahead of them were two lines of small lights that created a path toward the park.

"I told you this was far from over," Charles said. "If I get a chance to take you on a date, I'm going to capitalize on that."

"It's so pretty!" Avery squealed.

They started their walk along the light path. She felt warm fingers wrap through hers as he took her hand.

"Do you mind?" he asked sheepishly.

Avery shook her head.

He continued to tell her all about his life as a police officer before as they walked hand-in-hand through the path that meandered through the park. It had been a long time since Avery held anybody's hand. At the very least, Charles was her good friend. It felt comforting to her.

Eventually, they made it to the end of the path, and there, beneath a large, sprawling tree, was a dimly lit picnic blanket. Avery spotted an ice bucket and snacks waiting for them.

"How did you pull all of this together?" she asked.

Charles didn't answer. He simply led her to the picnic spot, and they sat down to enjoy a few glasses of bubbly together with some light snacks.

They stayed there for hours before their date was over. In the end, Avery learned that there was no expectation from her. All he wanted was her company, and it made her feel like the most special woman in the world. And that was a feeling she hadn't felt in a long time.

The End.

∽

Did you enjoy *Murder at the Wine Cave?*

If you loved this book, you'll definitely want to check out
Murder at the Grape Stomp!

Here's a sneak peek...

Enter a thrilling world of murder and mystery as innkeeper and
vineyard owner Avery Parker races against time to catch a
cunning killer during the annual grape stomp in picturesque Los
Robles, California.

With secrets, danger, and unexpected twists, indulge in suspense,
friendship, romance, and humor, complete with wine pairings
and irresistible recipes.

Turn the page to start the first chapter!

Local innkeeper and vineyard owner, Avery Parker, is having a blast with her friends during the annual grape stomp in their small town of Los Robles, California.

The air is filled with laughter, cheers, and the pulsating rhythm of stomping feet, creating an atmosphere that crackles with contagious energy.

But the good times come to a sudden end when a corpse is discovered in the vineyard.

Avery is stunned to learn that the motley collection of suspects includes a member of her own staff, who she had never considered a possibility.

As Avery uncovers the secrets behind the mystery, the stakes grow higher, threatening the safety of her employee and casting a shadow of danger over her own life.

With Sprinkles, her loyal golden retriever, by her side, Avery must navigate through tough decisions while seeking to solve the crime.

If the elusive murderer isn't found, Avery's very existence hangs in the balance, making every step of her investigation a heart-pounding race against time.

Murder at the Grape Stomp is a gripping tale of mystery that skillfully weaves together suspense, friendship, romance, and humor.

Wine pairings and irresistible recipes included!

~

Chapter One

I t was a moody day at Mountain Glaze Vineyard as their Fall Grape Stomp Festival went into full swing. Avery and the women of the Stammtisch wandered around the vineyard, comparing elements of it to Avery's vineyard, Le Blanc Cellars.

All around them, people were ankle-deep in grapes, stomping as hard as they could as children laughed and ran around them. It was a merry occasion that families seemed to enjoy. It was hard to believe it was the first grape stomp event Avery had attended since she set foot back in the Winelands.

The ladies had just finished their attempt at the grape stomp and were desperate for a place to sit and rest. But the festival was busy, and most seats were already taken. They would need to walk away from the crowd to find seating.

Avery enjoyed seeing what other vineyards looked like, and she enjoyed it most when she was with the Stammtisch. They were a small group of women who got together to socialize often. It wasn't something that Avery had ever expected to be a part of, but she was happy that she was. The women of the Stammtisch had been her best support more than once.

"See, they have a restaurant, too," Avery said, nudging Tiffany.

Tiffany sighed. She'd been Avery's best friend since school and had recently started working for Avery on the vineyard. But they'd been in an argument about opening a restaurant for some months already.

Avery felt she was missing out on something that every other vineyard had, whereas Tiffany felt like opening a restaurant would only create more work than any of them could manage.

For the most part, Avery trusted Tiffany's opinion without question, but she just could not shake the feeling that she was losing by not having somewhere for their visitors to enjoy a meal.

"I see the restaurant," Tiffany said quietly. "I also see how much work it is, too."

"Nothing I'm afraid of," Avery teased.

"That's because you've got me as your assistant," Tiffany laughed. "Then again, I know how stubborn you can be once you've made up your mind, and it is your vineyard to do with as you wish."

"You're absolutely right," Avery joked. "And right now, I wish for a restaurant!"

"I think it's a great idea," Eleanor chimed in.

Eleanor always had a way of showing up in a conversation precisely when she needed to. She was a smart and serious woman with a lot of ambition and the perfect kind of friend to have around when starting out on a new business venture.

"Thank you," Avery said. "Tiffany is right, it will be a lot of work. But everything I've done until now has been a lot of work, and it has all been worth it!"

"I agree," Tiffany said. "But we've only just started with the tasting area at the pond, and it's doing well. I'm only asking that you give it some time."

Avery smiled widely. "I'll think about it."

"You know what that means!" Eleanor joked. "Next week, the construction crew will arrive!"

Tiffany groaned and rubbed her temples as if she was getting a headache.

"Don't worry. I'll give you a head's up!" Avery joked.

Around them, the fall leaves of the vines glowed as the afternoon sun hit the earth. It was a beautiful, sprawling sight of reds, greens, and yellows that looked like a painting. For a moment, it felt to Avery as if she had stepped into a scene from a movie.

"What are you talking about?" Deb chirped as she rushed to keep up with them.

It was a phrase often heard escaping Deb's mouth. She was the group gossip. Deb could talk for hours about even the most boring topics, and she never missed an opportunity to learn something, especially if that information was pertaining to the lives of others.

"My boss is trying to work me to death," Tiffany said with a laugh.

"Is this about the restaurant again?" Deb asked. "Have you seen the one here? It's gorgeous! I wanted a bite to eat, but it is booked full."

"Did you hear that?" Avery said to Tiffany. "Booked full."

"Did you hear that the new Meat and Greet restaurant in town has closed?" Deb asked. "Apparently the owner's been pocketing most of the money instead of putting it back into the business."

"I never did like that guy," Tiffany mumbled.

"Everyone loved that place, so they'll be looking for a new place to go and eat. We're all bored of the few restaurants that Los Robles has to offer."

The women walked together, weaving between groups of running and excited children, all being closely followed by clumps of parents clutching their wine glasses. It was a perfect day with perfect views, and as she walked, Avery could feel the stresses of the previous weeks melting away.

All around them was laughter, chatter, and the sound of glasses clinking as strangers celebrated all their recent successes.

From the left, Camille giggled for reasons the rest of the women were unsure of. But that was not unusual. Camille was certainly the quietest of the group, and it was common for her to go hours without saying a single word. In fact, most of the time, the only contribution she made to conversation was a chuckle or a giggle in between others' comments. Camille was the ultimate observer, and because of that, Avery was sure she knew each of them better than anyone else.

She was a petite woman with a constant smirk on her face. Nobody really knew what she did for a living or who her family was. She'd never seemed willing to share, either. And yet, despite her silence, she was a big part of the Stammtisch, and they missed her terribly when she wasn't around.

The women of the Stammtisch did everything together. As the years passed, they became closer friends. It was completely different from the life that Avery had lived before. And often, when they hung out together, she reflected on her previous life.

Avery had been married to a successful crime writer and lived in the city. For all those years, she had been determined never to return to the small town of Los Robles where she had grown up. But then her husband died in a boating accident, and her life fell apart. She found it impossible to be in her city home without agonizing over her husband, who was missing from the space. In the end, she did move back to Los Robles and took over her parents' vineyard. Years later, she knew that it was one of the best things she ever did for herself.

It turned out that the life she had been trying so hard to avoid was the life she had been looking for all along. She had grown just as her vineyard did. Likewise, as her vineyard thrived and became a happier place to be, Avery found herself enjoying each day more and more.

Another thing that was different about her life was that she had Sprinkles, the golden retriever. She'd never seen herself as much of a dog person, but then again, as proven before, her parents knew her better than she did. In the end, she adopted the puppy to stop them from telling her to. Now a few years later, she hardly ever went anywhere without Sprinkles. Also, she'd given that dog the best life he could ever have.

As the women of the Stammtisch weaved their way through the festival crowd, Sprinkles stayed close by at her ankles.

"Let's enjoy this sun, ladies," Eleanor said. "Soon, it will be winter again, and I will be locking myself indoors out of fear of the cold."

The group passed a smart looking woman, who was well-dressed with sparkly jewelry decorating her, but as they got near her, Sprinkles started to growl at the woman. Avery tugged at his lead, embarrassed by his rude behavior.

Although he'd had schooling and was a well-trained dog, he occasionally growled at passersby, and Avery knew he was a good judge of character. More often than not, if he growled at someone, that person would end up being a shady character. So, Avery turned to take another look at the woman as she wondered why Sprinkles seemed distrustful of her. She was glamorous and seemed to know almost everybody there. Clearly, she was some kind of important figure in Brambles, the town they were in. Which only made Avery more embarrassed about Sprinkles' behavior. Thankfully, it seemed as if the woman was on her way out.

"Wine!" Eleanor cheered as she pushed a glass of chenin blanc into Avery's hand.

"Excellent," Avery agreed.

The women walked as they looked for a place to take a seat, but most of the seats were taken. Eventually, they spotted an empty table on the outskirts of the festival, right up against the vines.

Tiffany rushed over to claim it before anyone else could, and the tired women happily joined her there. By that point, they'd been walking around the festival for hours, and their feet were stinging.

"Thank goodness," Deb muttered as she sat down. "Ten more minutes, and I would have sat on the ground, and all of you would have had to help me back up again."

As they talked and laughed, Avery found herself grateful for the life she had and the day she had spent with the women. It felt like more than she could ever have asked for.

"How are things going between you and Charles?" Eleanor asked in her direction.

Avery smiled. "Things are going well. You know, it's still early days, and I'm not used to dating anymore. I was married for so long, so that's all I remember about dating. But Charles and I are having a lot of fun. And we're taking things slow."

"That's good!" Eleanor said with a smile. "What's it like dating a cop?"

It was a funny question, as Avery didn't really think of him as a cop. She still saw him as the man she knew when he worked in her wine shop. That was how they had met. He was a good man and someone who made her laugh.

Originally, Charles had retired from the police force, looking for another way of life. But in the end, he became a detective once more, wanting to help those who needed it. Once Avery was no longer his boss, he acted upon his stronger feelings toward her.

After he quit, they started spending even more time together. Avery was enjoying herself, but it had taken her a long time to feel comfortable moving on from her husband. In the end, it was easier than she thought it would be, and she didn't feel any of the guilt she'd expected to feel. Instead, she felt happy and excited to see him every time they had plans.

"I like Charles," Deb said. "He always makes me laugh."

"He is pretty funny," Eleanor agreed. "What's it like for him being back on the force?"

"He works way too hard, if you ask me," Avery said. "But he seems happy with it all. He enjoys solving crimes, you know? It gives him a kick."

"Well, you seem to have a thing for men who enjoy solving crimes. Charles just solves *real* crimes," Tiffany teased.

"I suppose you're right," Avery responded. "I haven't really thought about it like that, I guess."

"Which ones do you think are tougher to solve?" Deb asked. "The real ones or the ones in the books?"

"Oh, definitely the real ones," Avery responded quickly. "When you write a crime in a book, you're not actually dealing with real people. So, you can get away with anything. When you're solving a real crime, though, there are families involved who are desperate for answers. I think it is much tougher."

"That's a fair point," Deb said, getting a serious look on her face. "I mean, I *knew* that, obviously, but I haven't really thought about it much."

"Some days, I can see how much a case bothers Charles," Avery said. "But he always solves it, and that's the part that really matters."

"I guess you're learning a lot about the job by spending time with him," Eleanor said.

"Yes, like how much paperwork cops are required to do," Avery answered. "It's ridiculous. Never mind how much time he spends giving statements and answering questions in court."

As they spoke, Avery spotted a young couple walking hand-in-hand into the vines. She knew the look on their faces, and she was certain that they were newlyweds. They clung to each other as they walked, smiling and laughing, and she remembered her own honeymoon. She and her husband had looked just like that when they had walked together. She never expected things would turn out the way that they did.

She couldn't help but think that the couple had chosen an excellent spot for a honeymoon. It was also an excellent time of year. The vineyards were at their prettiest in the fall, and Los Robles and the surrounding towns featured many fall festivals that time of year.

Eventually, as the couple disappeared into the vines, Avery rejoined the conversation at the table, no longer knowing what anybody was talking about.

"I'm telling you," Deb said, "there is a world beyond this atmosphere that we can't even begin to imagine."

"Forget beyond the atmosphere!" Tiffany added. "We barely even know what's at the bottom of the ocean. That's what terrifies me most."

"And then there's the question of what comes after death," Eleanor joined in.

Clearly, Avery had missed a lot. She was about to ask them what they were talking about when a blood-curdling scream echoed out over the crowd, bringing the chatter to silence.

From within the vines, the screaming didn't stop.

Get *Murder at the Grape Stomp*
at your favorite retailer now!

Recipes

Breakfast Tacos (serves 4)

12 corn tortillas
2 tablespoon butter
8 large eggs
½ cup of Colby or Monterey Jack cheese, shredded (you can substitute with whatever cheese you have on hand)
½ cup cheddar cheese, shredded
4.5 ounces chorizo, removed from casing and pan fried
Salt and pepper to taste
Cilantro, chopped for garnish
Sour cream (optional)
Hot sauce (optional)

- Heat a large pan to medium-high.
- Prepare tortillas by frying in a non-stick pan, flipping occasionally until brown spots appear.
- Set aside and cover with tea towel to keep warm.
- In a medium bowl, whisk eggs and Colby Jack cheese until mixed well.

- In the same pan with medium-high heat, melt butter.
- Once butter is melted, pour egg and cheese mixture into the pan.
- As eggs are setting, use a spatula to move eggs from the outside of the pan toward the center.
- Continue moving eggs around until cooked to desired consistency.
- Season with salt and pepper to taste. Tent with aluminum foil to keep warm.
- To prepare the tacos, sprinkle two tablespoons of cheddar cheese on clean pan over medium heat.
- Place a tortilla on top of the melting cheese and cook until cheese crisps up and forms a crust.
- Remove from pan, fill taco with eggs, chorizo, cilantro, and sour cream (if desired).
- Serve immediately with hot sauce.

Pair with Michelada or sparkling wine

Michelada (serves 1)

Tajín seasoning
1 lime, cut into quarters
Clamato
3 splashes hot sauce (Cholula or Tapatio work)
2 splashes Worcestershire sauce
2 splashes soy sauce
12 ounce Mexican lager (Pacifico or Modelo beers are great here)

- Sprinkle a tablespoon of Tajin onto a small flat plate.
- Using a quartered lime, run it around the rim of a tall glass.

- Invert the glass onto the plate with Tajin to salt the rim.
- Fill the glass about a quarter of the way up with Clamato.
- Add remaining ingredients to the glass.

BBQ Chicken Pizza (serves 2)

Store-bought pizza dough (or make your own)
1 ½ cups leftover chicken, shredded
2 cups mozzarella cheese, shredded
½ cup of your favorite BBQ sauce (we like Sweet Baby Ray's at my house)
½ cup red onion, sliced
Cilantro, chopped for finishing

- Preheat the oven to 450°F.
- Bake the pizza dough for 6 minutes.
- Take out the dough and cover it with a layer of bbq sauce.
- Add a layer of sliced red onion and mozzarella cheese.
- Place shredded rotisserie chicken in a bowl.
- Pour a few tablespoons of bbq sauce over the chicken and toss everything together.
- Spread the chicken pieces over the pizza.
- Sprinkle an extra layer of cheese on top of the pizza.
- Add some chopped cilantro to your liking.
- Bake your pizza at 450°F for 10-15 minutes until the cheese is melted and the crust is golden brown.

Pair with malbec or zinfandel

Hearty Chicken Stew (serves 4)

1 yellow onion, diced
3 ribs celery, diced
4 cloves garlic, minced
½ pound carrots, sliced
1 ½ lbs. baby potatoes
2 lbs. boneless, skinless chicken thighs, cut into 1 inch pieces
4 tablespoons all-purpose flour, divided
2 tablespoons butter
1 tablespoon olive oil
1 teaspoon dried parsley
½ teaspoon dried thyme
½ teaspoon dried rosemary
½ teaspoon dried sage
¼ teaspoon freshly cracked black pepper
4 cups chicken broth
1 tablespoon fresh parsley, chopped for garnish

- Sprinkle 2 tablespoons of flour over the chicken, toss to coat.
- In a large pot, combine butter and olive oil over medium-high heat.
- When butter and oil are hot, add chicken.
- Brown chicken on all sides. Transfer chicken to a separate bowl.
- To the pot, add vegetables. Stir to cook on medium-high until onions are softened.
- Scrape up brown bits on the bottom of the pot as you sauté the vegetables.
- Once vegetables are softened, decrease heat to medium and add 2 tablespoons of flour. Cook for 2 more minutes.

- Add reserved chicken to the pot along with potatoes, herbs, pepper, and broth.
- Mix together while scraping off the stuck bits on the bottom of the pot.
- Cover the pot and bring to a boil. Remove lid, reduce heat to medium-low, and simmer for 30 minutes.
- Adjust salt to taste.
- Serve hot with sprinkling of parsley alongside crusty French bread.

Pair with pinot noir or red blend

Fudgey Fudge Brownies (serves 9)

12 tablespoons (1 ½ sticks) salted butter
2 tablespoons vegetable oil
¾ cup unsweetened cocoa powder
1 ¼ cup sugar
2 large eggs
2 teaspoon vanilla extract
¼ teaspoon salt
¾ cup all-purpose flour
½ cup chocolate chips

- Preheat your oven to 350 degrees Fahrenheit.
- Melt the butter in a large bowl using a microwave or a sauce pot.
- Whisk in cooking oil and cocoa powder until smooth.
- Add sugar to the mixture and whisk until evenly incorporated.
- Whisk in eggs, vanilla extract, and salt.
- Stir in flour until a thick batter forms.
- Fold in chocolate chips.
- Prepare an 8x8-inch baking dish by coating it with butter or non-stick spray.
- Add a piece of parchment paper (it doesn't need to cover all sides of the dish).
- Pour in the brownie batter and spread it evenly.
- Bake the brownies in the preheated oven for 40 minutes.
- Remove from the oven and let cool for 10 minutes.
- Lift the brownies out of the baking dish and slice into nine pieces.

Pair with cabernet sauvignon (preferably from Napa Valley) or merlot